A
Dean's
Life

Other Books By Robert Livingston

The Sailor and the Teacher

Travels With Ernie

Leaping Into the Sky

Blue Jackets

Fleet

Harlem on the Western Front

W.T. Stead and the Conspiracy of 1910 to Save the World

A Dean's Life

Robert Livingston

A DEAN'S LIFE

iUniverse books may be ordered through booksellers or by contacting:

iUniverse
1663 Liberty Drive
Bloomington, IN 47403
www.iuniverse.com
844-349-9409

ISBN: 978-1-6632-1932-9 (sc)
ISBN: 978-1-6632-1933-6 (e)

Print information available on the last page.

iUniverse rev. date: 03/10/2021

TO ALL THE WONDERFUL YOUNG TEACHERS

Contents

Introduction

"Yikes, me too!

Years ago I recalled standing in Powell Library on the UCLA campus peering at rows of doctoral dissertations in education, all cloaked in green binding and meandering through the overcrowded stacks with "pearls of wisdom." I realized, of course, that soon my thesis would join these dusty shelves, another attempt to satisfy a doctoral committee and perhaps to add to our collective wisdom. And that's when I said "me too."

As I gazed at this forest of academic research, I was struck by one question. Did any of these dissertations significantly improve teacher instruction and student achievement? My unsatisfying conclusion after 38-years in public education was very little.

Where had academia gone wrong? Certainly, not with the research; it was abundant and exhaustive. There was no question about the sincerity of the doctoral candidates. They were trying to improve things. Otherwise, what was the purpose of the whole enterprise? Was it merely to have a topic to appease doctoral requirements?

What then was the problem? The answer teased me in its simplicity. The potential of the research never reached the classroom teacher at the level of comprehension and adoption.

Partially, it was the pandemic writing style of research: incomprehensible syntax, inscrutable charts, and statistics designed to foster migraines. In the end it was a brew of hollow and tedious prose. That was the bitter truth.

It was the absence of any real connection by the research to a teacher's life in the classroom. It wasn't relevant. This was particularly true of new teachers. There was little to assist them in surviving their first few years so that they would make teaching a career. Having spent years in secondary schools, I was irrevocably convinced of that.

As I approached writing an irreverent survival guide for new teachers, I was determined to avoid such miscues. But how would I do that? I would have to think "outside of the box." I had to unshackle myself from conventional approaches to the problem.

Hopefully, I met this challenge through the retelling of mythic stories that display our humanity and enhance our empathic nature, and I did it by giving free reign to the comedic side of our personality. In other words, humor has a place in our lives and can be harnessed to help us survive the daily vicissitudes of the secondary classroom. Humor can be the lever by which we find not only introspection, but also a philosophical approach to life as a teacher. In this sense it helps to "carry on" regardless of the difficulties faced on a daily basis.

This is not a "here's what to do" manual promising success if you will follow the script. That would call for a "double yikes." Rather, it is more like a compass helping us to navigate our way. It is also an unapologetic biographical sketch of my life as a teacher and Dean and the lessons I learned in dealing with young people.

That said, one point should be made. For skeptics, this is not a "Pollyanna" approach. Rather, it is immensely serious, and fully appreciates our efforts to win "the hearts and mind" of our students.

Robert Livingston
2021

Chapter 1

False Alarm

"Crap"

What else could I say? Not the *S-word*, though I could feel it dangling on my lips. No, too messy, especially on a bright, warmish June day just before lunchtime on the high school campus. Anyway, not enough smack to it. Possible I could have used the *G-word*, but it took time since there was actually three words involved, *G-D-I.* And I didn't have time. Plus, I needed the Almighty on my side. Yes, crap was the best word for the circumstances I reluctantly found myself in. Sometime you just go with the flow.

"It will go off in thirty minutes."

That's what the frozen voice had said twenty-five minutes ago when I answered my phone in the Dean's Office at Van Nuys High School. A few words and the line went dead. "Why today?" I had asked then before calling in the bomb threat to my boss, Mr. Mendoza, the Assistant Principal.

"Just got a Double-O."
"Another bomb threat?"
"Yes."
"How long?"

"Thirty minutes."

"Activating Plan B."

"10-4"

Tall and lanky with very dark, black hair, Mr. Mendoza was a man of a few words, especially with the clock ticking. Of course, I knew what he meant. We had rehearsed this scenario often enough. Plan B: mobilize ten previously selected people to quickly search pre-determined areas of the high school campus for, as in this case, an assumed ticking bomb. Within two minutes ten civil servants scurried from their assigned duties and began their search, scrutinizing likely spots to place a bomb. The police and fire departments were also notified just in case.

Soon reports came in…

"Area 1 – nothing."

"Area 4 – clean."

"Area 8 – safe."

"Well, would you look at that," I said out loud to no one in particular, "I had to be the lucky guy."

I was staring at a cardboard box with a large *Apple* computer logo on it. The carton was half hidden under a pile of newspapers beneath the stairwell of A-Building, a two-story structure containing most of the English Department. Two stories… In a frenzy of hurried calculations, my feverish non-mathematical mind spewed out the unwelcomed numbers: 20 classrooms with an average of 30 students per class equals 600 kids at risk and at least twenty teachers. That's a lot of diagrammed sentences, misplaced modifiers, and dangling sentences shot to hell. Not a good situation.

"Area 2 – jackpot."

I checked my watch. Three minutes or less to go before the thing went off in my. That's when I said crap. I could have gone into a lengthy discourse on the injustices of the world, but there wasn't time. Succinctness was my style at this moment.

"Possible bomb, A Building, Area 2, I nervously repeated into my portable, brick-like radiophone that predated cell phones. "Under the west stairwell."

"Notifying first responders," Mr. Mendoza quickly said in response. "And watch the second hand!"

Funny how thoughts run through your head at times like this, my boss' admonishment notwithstanding. Had I set my watch correctly? Was it still keeping accurate time? I mean, what can you expect from a Rolex knock-off bought from a hustling vendor on Victory Boulevard? At the time, my $29.99 purchase seemed like a good investment, very stylish on a teacher's pay. Now, of course, a terrible thought crept into my consciousness. Did the crazy-voice have a more expensive watch, even a Neiman-Marcus special with a solid connection to the prime meridian running through good old Greenwich, England? Was I a second ahead or behind this nut case?" Timing was the key. In fact, it was everything. A second off might mean my state pension shot to blazes.

Less than two minutes now. The swirling second hand was sprinting across the watch dial, a stark black, plastic limb encased in shatterproof glass, mocking my futile attempts to stem its passage through time. Mr. Mendoza's agitated voice interrupted my musings.

"All units, "Code 004" now!"

Code 004 — no time left, clear the area, get out, back off, run like hell. Get into a open area. In short, forget the heroics. That's for the movies and we didn't work for United Artists or Warner Brothers.

"Livingston, respond!"
"10-4."

I was no screen hero. I knew my conservative dress suit and tie were not blast proof. Clearly, it was time to get my backside out of there. My fear-flight syndrome kicked in big time. I dashed away from the building and the mysterious Apple carton. I ducked behind a concrete planter where I noticed a cascade of beautiful spring flowers bursting brightly in the sunlight unconcerned with my plight. I awaited the will of the gods. What else can you do? Karma rules all.

The seconds ticked by, slowly now in rhythm with my pounding heartbeat now running on steroids. The remaining seconds passed, and then a another minute for good measure.

"Nothing!" I didn't know whether to cry or laugh as I yelled out the words, "Not a damn thing." Another false alarm and another silver hair atop my near retirement profile.

It was then that Mr. Mendoza arrived, a little out of breath from a long run across them campus. Others quickly followed as he said, "Let's check out the carton."

"Give it another hour."
"Dr. Livingston, always prudent."

I would have said "defensive," but one doesn't argue with the Assistant Principal at times like this. I compromised.
"Another minute to placate an old guy who wants to see his wife tonight."

That worked. Self-depreciation was always a useful tool in my survival kit.

Eventually we looked. Nothing. "Nada." Empty. Naturally, we were relieved. Our relief was tempered by one stark realization. Mr. Mendoza spoke for all of us, saying, "One of these days a bomb threat will be the real thing, or a gang-related gun threat will lead to a actual shooting. And then things will blow up in our scholarly faces."

"But not today, Mr. Mendoza," I quickly added.

He was right, of course. Each day we rolled the dice with potential violence as we tried to keep the lid on and the school safe. Was it Van Nuys High or Fort Apache? Truth be told, it was both at times.

"I need to get a memo out to the staff…"
"Don't leave empty cartons under stairwells?" I injected.
"Exactly."

At that moment our out-of-breath principal arrived, Dr. Russell Thomas. He was an ex-college offensive line football player. He was big and tough but a little out of shape for this business. He needed to get out of the Principal's Office more often. This, of course, I didn't mention to him.

"Where's the item?" he asked.

I pointed at the Apple carton.

"Looks innocent enough."
"So was the apple Eve gave Adam." I replied.

It's always good to have a biblical view of the world at times like this, I thought to myself.

"And looked what happened to Adam." I added, teasingly. "Took a bite and received an eviction notice."

"This principal is not in the mood for original sin."

Dr. Thomas liked to view himself in the third person. Not a problem for me.

"No matter," I continued, "with so much sin today, there's nothing original about it."

My principal wasn't into scripture today. He simply gave me a blank look.

As we stood there Officer Jose Rio arrived. Trained by the Los Angles Police Department (LAPD) he was our full-time, on-campus armed police officer. Husky and chunky, if one can be that simultaneously, he arrived with a beguiling look on his face.

"Just back from Court. Heard you had a bomb scare."

We just looked at him. I mean, what could we say?

Rio looked me in the eye, smiled, and then jabbed.

"One more adventure before you retire old guy. Seven years in the Dean's Office. This could be your big day. One last blast before you're pensioned off."
"Interesting choice of words, Rio."
"Isn't it?"

Now, what could I say? Five more days and I would be history, 60- years old, retired with a stamp-size photo in the school *Year Book*.

Chapter 2

Heroics

"Some hero."

The words just popped out. I was standing in my compact office in the main Administration Building, first floor, after lunch and the aborted bomb threat. For a moment I was alone. In a few minutes, a torrent of very upset, youthful offenders would be headed my way: those who were tardy to class too often, those who interfered with the teacher's instruction, and those who had slammed their hall locker too loudly or cursed their fate too strongly to be a teenager in society's holding pen, the public school. But for a moment I was alone with my thoughts.

"Some hero," I repeated.

I was staring unhappily at my reflection on a wall mirror. It was a small mirror in a rather small office bedecked with a large desk, my padded chair on wheels, and three hard, very uncomfortable wooden chairs to temporarily seat upset kids and parents. A small computer table holding a spanking new PC was adjacent to my desk. Three cabinets were against one wall. They were loaded with student files recalling the misadventures of those who figured out ways to get into trouble. This was my little world stranded on light brownish floor tiles with a decidedly unappetizing institutional look. A bank of stark fluorescent lights hovered harshly above all, illuminating, but not always enlightening those below. The room's saving grace was a wonderful picture window, which provided an expansive view of shrubs, trees, grass, and a parade of flourishing roses, as well as outside busy street fronting the school. Facing eastward, the window invited the morning sun and the rebirth each day of public education, and for the Dean's Office a multitude of challenges.

The mirror stared back at me, a willing conspirator in reflecting an uncompromising reality; it didn't need sodium pentothal to extract the truth from it. The visage before me negated that need. I'd like to say I saw a handsome, somewhat macho face peering back at me with lively blue eyes, a stout chin, and a hairline closer to my eyes than my ears, a stylish fellow in his late 40's, still slim and athletic. That was not to be. No *Esquire Magazine* look clamored for my attention. Not even *Popular Mechanics*. Instead, a craggy, ruddy-lined face with hazel-colored eyes, and a receding hairline with specks of gray glared back at me with a somewhat philosophical continence, as if to say, "Sorry bud, this is the best I can do." That was code, I assumed, for age-creep as I approached the "big 60" and momentarily, self-imposed retirement.

The mirror hinted at more, especially around the eyes. I had been afraid today. That silent admission did not come easily for me. I preferred to think of myself in more heroic terms, stud-like if you wish, something between John Wayne and Burt Lancaster keeping peace in Waco. But heart of heart, that wasn't the case, not at all. I hadn't wanted to find the elusive bomb. Like tiny beads of perspiration, nervousness had coated my being, leaving me almost uncontrollably anxious as I searched for the damned bomb. It had taken an immense effort to do my job. Fear, you know, can do that to you.

What was going on? Deep down I knew. I, as I said earlier, was retiring after 38-years in the school district. My NEA membership would soon be replaced by an AARP affiliation, as would my sporty little Mazda 3 by a late model RV for promised treks across America with my wife of almost four decades. Over the past six weeks a gnawing gut feeling had invaded my consciousness, a kind of premonition that violence lurked in the near future. I couldn't disavow the feeling, nor could I jettison it to the scrap heap of unhappy thoughts. The feeling stuck to me like a first class stamped notification from a persistent collection company.

Of course, violence on school campuses was sadly nothing new. With a high school population approaching 4,000 students, Van Nuys High was actually a small town. That said, there was a need for a uniformed officer and a Dean's Office to maintain security on campus (make that law and order). Nothing stopped at the school door, neither the joys of the larger society, nor the unhinged behavior of some. The potential for violence was a constant shadow and it was getting to me as some recent events indicated.

Gun Deal

While practicing for the graduation ceremony on the football field, a few days ago a young man ran up to me, out of breath, and nearly shouting.

"Dr. Livingston, there are three guys with a gun."
"Where?"
"By the baseball field."
"I'll check it out. Keep it to yourself. No need to start a panic. Understand."

That's me, Gary Cooper in High Noon about to face down the bad guys. I'd like to think I took off at full speed, encountered the bad guys, disarmed them without a shot, and brought them before the local sheriff for their just desserts. Well, that's not necessarily what happened. Here's what did take place. Using my brick-phone, I called in the alert to Officer Rio and then headed toward the ball field at my old-man gait. As I got closer to the field, I slowed to a cautious half-trot. I saw three guys huddled together as if they were making a deal, possibly a drug deal. At about fifty yards the three guys spotted me lumbering toward them. A moment later I recognized two of them, students from our school, but not the third person, who took off like an Olympic sprinter. So what was going on? According to the two boys, the runner was also a seller, but not drugs. Rather, he was peddling a realistic looking air pistol. This I called into the Officer Rio, suggesting that he not overreact if he encountered the seller (not a killer). All in all things worked out, but that wasn't a given. What if a real gun had been involved? What if the seller in panic had fired away? Goodbye Gary Cooper. Hello "boot hill." Those morbid thoughts rummaged through my mind leaving me in a cold sweat.

Intimidation

Earlier in the semester a flustered student caught up to me in the Main Office, clamoring about someone with a gun in front of school. As always, I followed routine. I alerted others and exited my office. I went out the front door of the school. It was almost time for the 3 o'clock bell to end the school day. A crowd of parents and students were already milling around outside of the school. I searched the crowd for a guy with a gun. The other Dean, a likeable fellow by the name of Jenks, joined me. And yes it's true; he was youthful, athletic, and a prone to action guy. He spotted a possible suspect and charged into him while I provided backup from a discrete distance. Somewhat unsteadily, but certainly cautiously, I watched the encounter. It turned out this guy did have a gun. He was determined to intimidate a student about a drug deal gone wrong. The gun, however, was inoperable, but that wasn't known until later. Again all turned out well. Of course, questions did arise, festering in my beleaguered brain and dissatisfying sense of doom. What if the guy's gun was operable? What is the other Dean had been shot? What would I have done? Once more, I envisioned myself as taking on the OK Corral, but, if I were you, I wouldn't bet the house on that. The best I can say is this; I would have tried to do my job.

By now you can see I was just trying to hang on, sort of like a trapeze artist avoiding a misstep. Just a few more days; certainly enough time for anything to happen, and more than ample time for me to reflect on how I ever ended up in the Dean's Office.

Chapter 3

Ballots and More Ballots

I think it all began with the teacher strike of 1989. That business sealed my fate. I decided to run for the chairmanship of our local union that year. Don't ask me why. I couldn't give you a cogent answer. I simply threw my hat into the ring.

"Why are you running for union rep?" the school's print shop teacher asked.

"I think I would be a good union leader," I responded. "I'm ready to lead our school into this strike."

"You sure you know what it takes?"

"Leadership?"

"You can keep the faculty together?"

"I can try."

Talk about an ideal candidate, giving strong, direct answers to pointed questions, straying away from benign, incipient, nuanced responses. If only that were the case...

We were in the music room after school holding a UTLA union meeting (United Teachers of Los Angeles) to elect a new school union representative, a Rep. About 100 teachers were in attendance to hear what the candidates, including myself, had to say. Upset and anxious about the impending strike, the faculty was challenging us with tough questions. They wanted to make sure their new leader was up to the job. Who could blame them?

Going into the race, I was generally considered a long shot, a dark horse. I was in the Social Studies Department teaching mainly US Government and Economics to seniors, and occasionally two elective classes, Comparative Religions and Psychology. It's always nice to have an in with Moses and Sigmund Freud, even if the relationship was somewhat tenuous. I also presided over the Student Council, but that was about it except for a couple of faculty-students shows to raise funds. Of course, I had participated in the first painful strike in 1970, almost twenty years earlier, which I shared with the faculty. We had won a favorable contract only to have it declared null and void by the California Supreme Court. Unfortunately, the state had no law permitting public employees to strike at that time. That was not the case now.

As to why there was an election at this time. Surprisingly, Old Man Reilly, who had been the union Rep for nearly a decade, was throwing in the towel on the eve of the strike after years of strong leadership. Maybe, I later thought, he knew something.

Teacher strikes are bad news. For most teachers, they are going against that which gave meaning to their lives, classroom instruction and wonderful interactions with their students. To withhold their labor of love was like cutting off an arm regardless of the pent-up economic grievances motivating the strike. There would be no joy on the picket line, only degrees of regret mixed with anger and frustration.

Yes, as I said, maybe Old Man Reilly knew something.

Teachers, by experience and education, are not militant folks. They tend to be on the conservative side. They relish consistency and predictability. They like structure. Chaos is no friend. They rejoice in positive relationships with their students and the parent community.

In short, they find volatile, combative, and an "in your face" attitude unappealing. It's just not in the DNA of their teacher certificate.

Teachers may belong to a union but they don't have the passion and resolve of dockworkers, steel workers, and coal miners. They may have a sense of injustice, but they lack the anger that comes from heavy physical labor and bosses who, all too often, could care less about "due process" and the niceties of law. Teachers, bolstered by their academic prowess and parchment degrees, want to be liked and respected for their profession and intellect. Unlike the Teamsters, they don't want to be feared. They don't want to be seen as tough-as-nails blue-collar stiffs fighting for a respectable salary to care for their families. They knew the union chants, but they lacked the heart to rip justice from their "betters."

The questions continued; I tried to reply with catchy answers.

"I never thought of you as a militant," a feisty math teacher commented. "Christ, you wear a suit and tie in the classroom. Hell, you look like an administrator."
"Guilty as charged, but my garb suits me."

My play on words died in a din of groans. I tried to redeem myself.

"But I wear a *Eugene V. Debs* button on my jacket lapel."
"Really?" asked an agreeable middle-aged music teacher.
"Never heard of him" cried a muscled P.E. teacher.
"He was a kind of coach" I retorted. "On our side."
"Well, you still look like one of them," said Mr. Feisty, the math teacher, who continued to complain.

For the uninitiated, 'them' referred to management, the administrative staff, and the protagonists in this play.

"Looks can be deceiving," I said quietly.

I wasn't fooling anyone. Compared to the other candidates, I was coming across as soft, as not militant enough. Earlier, I had opposed putting glue in all the school locks once a strike vote passed. I was opposed to overtly recruiting students to picket with us, and unwilling to push young teachers with emergency credentials to walk the line with strikers unless the union would protect them. I didn't want them to lose their jobs. In good faith I couldn't jeopardize their future livelihood.

"What's your platform?" a bookish colleague and sympathetic friend from the History Department asked.

What was my platform? Should I tell my colleagues I was a weary history teacher tired of talking about history in the classroom and desirous of making some? Some plank; it sounded like Ego 101. Truth to be told, however, after so many years in the classroom, I was bored silly. I needed some action. I needed a fight. I needed to put on some boxing gloves and go at it with the Board of Education, the great Satan in this drama. Naturally, I didn't divulge these motivations. The faculty wanted a strong leader, not a psycho.

"I'm prepared to do three things."

Talk about an expansive platform. My words fell like on deaf ears, much like the lame student excuse, "My dog ate my homework."

"Such as what?" a white-coated science teacher with thick glasses blared out in less than a friendly way.
"Yeah, what?" a suspicious Special Education instructor asked.

This was it. I could count to three, but did I really have three issues. If so, one of them had taken flight. Anyway, it was time to wing it.

"First, I'll help you to close down the school, 100% if possible."
"Close down the school?"
"Absolutely. No instruction."
"How?"

"Convince everyone to strike."

"You haven't met some of the guys in the P.E. department. Practice and games, that's what they care about…"

"Yes, but they'll sure take the raise. We must still try to enlist their assistance."

"Good luck with that one."

This was not a happy crowd. I wasn't winning many converts. Custer had it better at the *Little Big Horn*.

"What about scabs?" What should we do about them?"

"Scratch them."

The room was silent. Once more my rhetorical efforts at levity hadn't swayed the crowd.

"You're kidding."

"Yes, I'm kidding."

"Well?"

"Simple proposition. If you're not going to physically stop them from entering the school, which would lead to a police response, the only thing we can do is let them pass."

"Let them pass?"

"You can hoot if you want."

"Hoot?"

"Well then, gesture."

"Gesture?"

"OK, I get the picture. You want a more aggressive action."

"Yes."

That's what the faculty wanted. They wanted to man the ramparts and bludgeon the enemy. The *Marseillaise* was in their veins.

How far should I go? When you're the underdog, you really have nothing to lose but your pride, your sense of self-esteem, or your belief in yourself. Easy. Just let it all hang out.

"Aggressiveness? That's what you want? Okay. Here's what you do. Buy a fifteen inch length of metal pipe, wrap it with newspapers, good and thick, and tie it all together with heavy rubber bands."

"That's being aggressive?"

"Then bring that pipe to school and slam every car hood driven by a scab. Hit the headlights. If that's what you want to do, I'll make a quick run to Home Depot. Any takers?"

"You would do that?" the school nurse asked.

"I was raised in San Francisco. I'm a disciple of the Harry Bridge's 'School of Negotiations", which is beloved by longshoreman everywhere. "Whack, bang, boom…" Yes, if the faculty will put up my bail."

"Really?"

"Really!"

The room was quiet. Not a sound. As expected, there were no takers. Teachers aren't into the physical stuff. Fortunately, the topic was temporarily dropped.

"What else?"

"What else what?" I asked.

"What's your second point?"

"Second, I'll plan our strike strategy."

"Meaning?"

"I'll coordinate our picketing schedule, before and after school."

"Picket signs?"

"Of course. And we'll march in a dignified and disciplined manner to ward off, if possible, the scabs, and to win over parents.

"No lead pipes?"

"No lead pipes."

Nothing to lose now, I figured. Either the faculty goes for this or it doesn't.

"What's the third thing?"

What was the third thing? For a moment I felt like a deer in the headlights, or virginal boxer stepping into the ring with Mohammad Ali. Then I had it, but would the faculty buy it? And would I be able to do it?

"I'll ask you to stay out if you go out, and, when the strike is over to return to work without fratricide."

"Fratricide! What are you talking about?"

"Strikes can tear our faculty to shreds with anger. Some folks will go out initially, but be unable to stay out if the strike is lengthy. Some will not go out at all. If we win a contract, all will benefit, strikers and non-strikers. Can we return to work leaving vindictiveness behind, or will retribution color our feelings and divide the faculty into warring groups?

This was it. I would win or lose the union election based on what I was about to say.

"Ideally, we want every teacher to go out and stay out, but that's not possible in the real world. Some faculty members, no matter their best intentions, will not be able to stay out. The personal and financial stress will be too much."

"Well then they are scabs."

"No, they're folks who did their best. They're not scabs. They're our friends and colleagues."

"But they will harm the strike."

"That's true, but when this thing is over with we have to work together. No grudges, no department fissures, no fist fights in the heads."

"You're too soft for this job."

"Maybe, but think about this. What good will it do to win the strike and lose the war by coming back to a school torn apart by anger and ill will?"

During the next two weeks, the faculty debated the candidates running for office, and then voted. Surprisingly, I came in first by a scant few votes, and later in the school year, after a twelve-day strike, the union won a very favorable contract — 10% per year for three years. In addition to a healthy pay raise and improved medical benefits, there was an almost unnoticed provision in the contract for the future elections of Deans by the faculty. This provision would replace the traditional principal-appointment system currently in use. No longer could the Principal appoint a favorite, a proven loyalist, someone going into administration, and who would support the administration's policies without question. The faculty would elect a fellow faculty member.

As expected, a few teachers left the picket line and returned to the classroom. And predictably, a few hardliners never forgave them for doing so. As for the scab-substitutes, no tires were slashed, no fists were thrown, and no ring scratching occurred. Certainly, the middle finger was exercised frequently in silent protest, a political gesture of a sort, to let people know how we felt. I must admit I was tempted by this non-verbal communication, but alas, as the Union Rep I could but think the thought. I needed to be a role model, a calming influence in chaotic waters. Inside my jacket, I sometimes gave into temptation, but that's our little secret.

Each day we picketed in the morning and afternoon. We had the *AM Gang* and the *PM Gang* with each group supplemented by parents and students (unorganized, of course), and a continuous supply of doughnuts, soft drinks, and a bit of morale rhetoric by me to keep the troops encouraged and disciplined. By the time the strike ended, I was on a first name basis with every teacher, and future voters.

I guess I did O.K. A few weeks after the strike ended, the faculty presented me with a token of its appreciation. It was a beautiful glass apple perched on a wooden and plastic foundation with a lovely sentiment.

TO THE HEAD-LINER
DR. BOB
WITH THANKS FROM, THE PICKET-LINERS
VNHS 1989

About this time, I decided to run for a Dean position if one became available under the new contract. And one day one did. One of the Deans transferred to another school. An opening existed. I intended to fill it.

"I don't believe it."

Those were my delighted words six months later when the faculty elected me Dean after a bruising campaign against two other more macho candidates. Again, tough questions had come up during the campaign:

"Are you sure you can keep up with these kids?"
"Unless they're on roller skates, yes."
"You're not seen as a disciplinarian?"
"My classes are under control."
"You don't raise your voice. Will the kids in trouble listen to you?"
"We'll just have to see."
"But you've never had any Dean experience before."
"Not quite true. I worked in the Deans Office in a middle school and in another high school before I came here."
"We didn't know that."

One election victory had led to another. After almost thirty years of surviving in the classroom, I was taking up residence in the Dean's Office via the secret ballot, a gift of the new contract. And that's how I got a small office with a big picture window.

Chapter 4

Job Actions

"I had to run for UTLA Rep."

The words trembled into the air as I strolled toward the Boy's PE Office, heart in hand. You'll recall the faculty warned me about the PE teachers, suggesting they would not go on strike. Though that might prove the case, as the Union Rep I had to make a good faith effort to enlist their support. With that in mind, I arranged for before school meeting with all the PE teachers, very possibly grudging guys and gals (I do have a weakness for alliteration). To tell the truth, I felt like the man who had an appointment in Samarra.

Storming the PE Bastion

Ten PE teachers who were also coaches waited for me. To their credit they greeted me with friendly smiles, and by all appearances open to what I might say. They had, however, already made up their minds. I knew that. They would not strike. That became abundantly clear from the outset.

"We're not going out," a muscular weightlifting coach said as I sat down.
"That's not why I'm here."

"You're the Rep."

"True, but I'm here for a different reason."

That got them. They had expected a call to arms by me, or at least to run a guilt trip on them. I was doing neither. So why was I in their office?

"Well, why are you here?" an impatient lady volleyball coach quickly asked.

"Numbers," I said. "Numbers."

More questioning looks.

"What are you talking about?" the tall, lanky men's basketball coach inquired.

"Ratios."

By now I was sounding like a math teacher. I was also sounding mysterious. That was okay with me. People were tuned in, I hoped, not turned off.

"A little history, folks. During the 1970 strike a myth was perpetuated by the administration that the schools were open and functioning though two-thirds of the faculties were pounding the pavement. They sold that line to the public. True the schools were open, but who was supervising the students with so many teachers out?"

I had posed the question. Now it was time to answer it.

"PE teachers were asked to supervise three to four times the number of student they usually had, which was already a large number. Instead of 1 to 50 for a regular PE class, it was now 1 to 200 or more kids. In other words, the PE teachers took up the slack supervising holding tanks. It's all a matter of record."

"The Rep has that right. My uncle was coaching soccer at that time. He didn't even take roll. Kids were herded into the football stadium where they sat until the smarter ones simply left campus."

"You think that will happen again?" the baseball coach asked, looking directly at me.

"Guaranteed."

It was quiet for a moment as things sank in. That couldn't last and didn't.

"What is it you want?"

This was the tricky part. One mistake here and javelins and shot puts might come my way. To survive I would need to be as smooth as delightful New England syrup.

"I know you have coaching responsibilities. Those must be honored in the world of competitive athletics. You are also PE teachers and will be on campus. I ask only one thing of you. To the extent you can, please avoid the dumping process. In 1970 that was a factor in prolonging the teacher strike. If possible, try not to cover three or four combined History or English classes. In other words, contribute to the job action in this important manner."

"You want us to disobey the Principal?"

I gave a lawyer's answer.

"Subject to the current contract and the State Code, do what you can to help your fellow teachers."

"You want an answer now?"

"No. That's not required now or later."

"What will you tell the faculty?"

"Only this; we discussed the matter."

The strike occurred. The PE teachers didn't strike. But they made uneven efforts to watch the numbers. In an imperfect world that was enough, I think. Survival is not always easy.

Nasty Little Secrets

Almost without saying, if you become a teacher, you'll end up in a job action at some point. A few things to keep in mind when that happens:

Secret #1 - Strikes are not inevitable. The heavens do not ordain them.

Secret #2 - Strikes are a public confession that management (the Board of Education) and workers (UTLA in this case) failed to address employee grievances.

Secret #3 - With respect to salaries and medical benefits in particular, both sides know in advance — within a percentage point — what they can live with. There are no bookkeeping secrets. Sleight of hand and hyperbole, false claims, and unfounded criticism maybe, all to win the favor of the public, but that's about it.

Secret #4 – Both management and labor need an occasional job action to justify their existence tied to collective bargaining. Each side must prove to its constituencies the righteousness of its position. Management must act tough. The next election is around the corner. Labor has the same challenge. Caught in the middle of this dance are three groups, parents, teachers, and students.

"Secret #5 – Unless extremely fortunate, most faculties cannot weather a job action without a degree of hard feelings. It's the natural outcome when strikers and non-strikers each receive the same benefits of the job action. It sometimes takes years to heal such schisms.

Where does that leave the average teacher, assuming such a creature exists? The answer is unsatisfying. Teachers are caught in the middle. They understand the *pencil phenomenon*. Take one pencil and break it. Not difficult. Easily done. Take a hundred pencils... That's much more difficult to break. Teachers are many things. They are also pencils. Given that, they must find a way to survive, in a world of collective bargaining, nasty little secrets notwithstanding.

Chapter 5

Initiation

"What do I do now?"

I repeated the question numerous times following my election victory. Over the weekend between semesters I had to prepare myself for the Dean's Office. Would I be ready?

Unfortunately, there was no *Dean's Office for Dummies* book available at my local Borders Bookstore. The school district published no guidebook. Nor did it conduct a seminar for newly elected Deans. Essentially, I was on my own.

The Principal had proffered me a tight-tongued word of congratulation, saying, "Well, good luck." Mr. Mendoza, my immediate boss, uttered a quiet, "I wish you the best." As for my future colleague, Don Jenks, he seemed to take my ascendancy in stride with a friendly refrain, "Let me know if you need any help." Officer Rio, however, was suspicious. I think he wondered whether I had the makings of a good cop, which was the way he perceived a Dean. I can't blame him. He had asked me a number of questions during a brief encounter twenty-four hours earlier.

"Do you know what 'BVN' stands for" Mr. Dean?"
"BVN?"

"Is there an echo in the room?"
"No sir."
"Well?"
"It's a gang, isn't it?"
"Ah, you do know something."
"Barrio Van Nuys?"
"Correct."

I knew what the letters meant but very little else. BVN was our school's only gang, a sort of generational fraternal organization in the local mainly Hispanic neighborhood. I had heard rumors about it, but nothing solid. Supposedly, its members were given to after school criminality, including physical stuff when required. On campus, its membership claimed certain campus real estate, and was not above shaking down new students, especially those who might have other gang affiliations, with one penetrating question, "Where're you from?"

The truth was I knew very little about gangs, but I would learn. The real world always imposes upon ignorance. Rio prompted continued his interrogation.

"What do you know about drug activity on campus?"
"Most of the teachers could use some."
"Probably right, but that wasn't the question."

I tried to be funny to loosen up the impromptu inquisition. Rio was not having any of it. Trained by the Los Angeles Police Department, he was the man, and I was going to learn that.

"I thought so," he said with distain. "Well, what about district rules concerning drugs?"
"Students shouldn't use them during finals?"
"Jesus."

Rio's face indicted he was not interested in my attempts at levity. "Christ," he said, "don't you know anything?"

"Yes, a little, but don't worry Officer Rio, I'm a fast learner so let's knock off the Q and A. You'll teach me what I need to know. That's your job, isn't it?"

I blustered to cover my limited drug IQ. Sometimes blustering was good. Rio responded as I had hoped.

"School begins next week. We'll see if you're really a fast learner."
"I'll be here bright and early."
"God help us."

Not to be deterred by Rio's proclamation, Jenks, my fellow Dean, now got into the picture to remind me of my novice standing, the new kid on the block.

"Know anything about our detention policies?"
"They detain people?"
"Funny man."

No smile, not even a smirk. Jenks wasn't having any of my humor. He was going to show me he was a hard assed guy.

"Referrals to continuation schools?"
"They follow high school?"
"Still with the smart answers."

I decided to alter the conversation.

"They provide an alternative school setting for those students who have used up their welcome Van Nuys?"
"Well, well, you do know something."
"A few things."
"What about suspensions and opportunity transfers?" And for that matter, expulsions?"

"We remove students to support the integrity of the instructional program, or to safeguard individuals when the situation requires such action consistent with district policies and the California State Code of Education."

"It seems you do know something."

"I've picked up a few things through the years kicking around in the classroom and doing a few odd jobs."

I decided it was time to bluster again.

"Listen Jenks, you're the lead guy here, as is the Officer. But I'm no kid. I'm over half a century old so I expect a little respect, at least for my age. Have you got that straight or do I need to repeat myself?"

Once more, blustering did the trick. Being indignant can be a nice survival technique. Jenks, a little shook up, responded as desired.

"O.K., age has its place."

"Right," I said, "especially in my office adjacent to your stall."

"O.K., Mr. Tough Guy, you've made your point."

"Here's another one. I was once a Dean, years ago."

A startled Jenks said, "What?" A bemused Officer Rio couldn't believe his ears, saying, "No way."

For once, I wasn't bordering on provocation. This was no fictionalized claim, though not totally the truth, what we might call stretching the facts, a kind of *Plastic Man* reach. But I had been an assistant to the Dean in both a middle and senior high school. That was history.

The Middle School

I was in my second year of teaching back in the early 60's. The Principal, Ben Werner, asked me one day if I was interested in gaining administrative experience. In my usual unequivocal manner, I answered, "Sort of." He suggested I work in the Deans Office one period each day for a start. "Of course," he pointed out, "you'll give up your conference period to do this. You'll still have your regular teaching assignment."

"I'll give it a try."
"Good. I think you'll like it."
"I'm not too inexperienced?"
"No, we like young people helping out."

Though he didn't say it, I later figured out what was going on. Assigning young teachers to school offices provided no costly labor, since their conference periods were being used for this purpose. It was a sort of indentured servitude, self-afflicted. Be that as it may, one did get experience. Mine began with swats administered in the Deans Office.

Swats

In those days, swats were given to boys for unacceptable behavior. Girls need not apply; they were off limit. Swats were only given after calling the parent, explaining the situation, and recommending a swat. If the parent agreed, it was done. If not, other action was taken. The Office had a complete set of paddles, large, small, and intermediate depending on the backside size of the culprit in question. A certain ritual was taken when a swat was given. To begin with, the boy was asked to assume the position, which meant he faced a wall, placed his hands on it, and bent forward. After that, the Dean patted down his back pockets to make sure no hard object was present like a key chain, coins, or a ballpoint pen. A swat hitting those items caused real pain. A whack with the paddle was bad enough.

In those days, a swat was legal and parents mainly supported your action. Today, it would be considered a form of *"water boarding"* by some. A legion of *"Sue them now, sue them big"* would be in court before the school day ended. The Dean and my boss, Mr. Black, always wanted me to apply the paddle. His name seemed to describe his view of the world and student offenders. For him, it was a sort of test. Did I have the stomach to be a Dean? As it turned out, I did. I could, when asked, apply a swat, but I did so with no great relish except on some occasions when events tickled my funny bone.

Case #1 – The Cover-Up

"This kid needs a swat. I've called home. No problem with the family."

"Right. What was his crime, Mr. Black?"

"He was too interested in Mrs. Lovelace's purse."

"The geometry teacher?"

"She caught him red handed."

"Where is the kid?"

"Joey? He went to the bathroom. Give him a good one."

A good one… That meant our specialty paddle, the one with holes drilled out of it for greater whacking power. I never understood the physics of it, but the results were always the same, a more compact, stinging swat for your money.

Eventually Joey returned from the restroom. He surprised me by his attitude.

"I'm ready for my swat."

"No objections?"

"No. I'm ready."

"You know why you're getting a swat?"

"Mrs. Lovelace's purse?"

"Opening it up."

"I was only looking."

"For?"

"I don't know."

"Money?"

Joey didn't answer me. He stared at the floor lips tightly closed. He would teach me, as others would, that kids can lie with a straight face, or least distort the truth to their advantage with a remarkable stage presence. As a youthful skill, it didn't always help much in the Deans Office, but it might prepare you for political office. "Look out Mr. Mayor. You've got a budding rival." In this case, Joey figured I was on to him. He didn't deny his actions, nor did he defend them. He simply accepted his fate.

"Let's get this over with. I'm prepared."

"I like your attitude, Joey. You're handling this like a man. Assume the correct position against the wall."

With that, he did. I patted him down. Almost immediately I realized something was wrong. The pat didn't feel right. Then I had it. Joey had padded himself with paper towels in the restroom. He had done a very nice job. The padding was smooth, providing no hint of its presence. He wanted to cushion the blow. Smart kid.

"Joey, are you wearing thick underwear today?"

"The usual."

The usual... This kid was good. Who was he trying to fool? I couldn't restrain myself. I started to smile, then to laugh inwardly at the ingenuity of this kid. No wonder he was ready. But what should I do? That was the question. Should I send Joey back to the restroom to de-towel? No way. Joey might turn into an 8th-grader flight risk. No, it was better to deliver his just reward. I grabbed the holed paddle, backed away further than usual, and prepared to take a Babe Ruth swing at the kid.

"Ready?"

"Yes."
"Don't move."

I took my swing aiming to knock the ball out of the park. The paddle collided with Joey's backside to a resounding "puff" sound. I felt like I had just slammed into a pile of disposable diapers. "Puff." A wall of towels and air absorbed the whack leaving the kid relatively untouched. "Puff." Again, I couldn't resist it. A smile grew on my face and then a hearty laugh.

"Damn. That was like hitting a wall of super-sized *Pampers*.

Joey didn't say a word. We talked for a few minutes about cleaning up his act in Mrs. Lovelace's class, which meant a letter of sincere apology to her, co-signed by his parents. Also, he was admonished to stop exploring his teacher's purse. Another incident would be a police matter. He nodded in agreement. As he left the Office for in-house detention, I said, "Nice one." He responded with a slight hint of a smile and was gone. To my knowledge his purse-viewing days ended.

Case "#2 – Peer Pressure

On another occasion Steve, a seventh-grader rushed into the Office with a huff and handed me a referral slip from Mr. Merritt, the music teacher, which I quickly scanned.

"Do you know why you're here, Steve?"
"Yes."
"Tell me."
"I threw a spit wad at my friend."
"One spit wad?"
"Three."
"Busy day."
"I was defending myself."
"Defending yourself?"

"He fired first!"
"You retaliated?"
"Whatever."
"He didn't get caught?"
"Because?"
"My aim was off. I hit Mr. Merritt."
"On purpose?"
"No. I told you. I overthrew."
"Happens."
"What are you going to do?"
"What do you think I should do?"

With that, Steve clammed up. In cases like this, the usual protocol called for a a parent conference, by phone and the ubiquitous letter of apology. All this I shared with Steve.

"No, he said."
"No?"
"I want a swat."
"What?"
"I want a swat."
"This situation doesn't require a swat."
"You don't understand."
"Explain."

So he did … Outside of the Office were seated three of his spit wad buddies, all of whom expected him to get a swat. If he did, he would be a respected member of their club, *The Swatters* or something like that.

"Please," he said.

I gave the kid a long look. There was no rule to cover this one.

"What the hell."
"What?"

"This is the deal Steve. I'll still call home. You still write a note of apology, and I'll give you a swat."

"Thanks. This means a lot to me."

"I can see that."

"Should I assume the position? My friends told me what to do."

"No."

"No?"

"I'll whack the table, and you yell and do the swat dance as you leave the Office. Got it? We'll fool your friends. It will be our secret."

"Really?"

"Yes."

"Cool."

The Indian dance was the final ritual of the swatting experience. A good swat left a temporary hot, burning sensation on the "seat of learning." A student didn't walk away from a swat. He hopped as he held his hands on his still stinging rear.

And so I whacked the table and Steve yelled like crazy before grabbing his butt and dancing out of the room. As he left, he gave me a wink and was my best buddy for the next two years. To my knowledge, he never threw another spitball in Mr. Merritt's class. As to his other classes…

Case #3 – Deceiving Looks

David was a nice kid, a special education seventh-grader who had been encouraged by older kids to set off a fire alarm. An observant teacher caught him in the act and brought him by the ear to me. This was serious business. Classes are disrupted by false fire alarms. Firemen have been killed in traffic accidents while responding to alarms.

"What were you thinking, David?"

"I don't know."

"Did others put you up to this?"
"Yes."
"Who?"

David didn't answer me.

"I need to know. All of you are going to be suspended." David didn't say a word. He just smiled at me.

"Did you hear what I said? You guys are in big trouble."

Again, there was no verbal response from David. He only looked at me with a bigger smile or was it a smirk? Either way I didn't like it. This time there was also some twitching in his chair. He couldn't, it seemed, sit still. There were no denials from David. No protests. Nothing.

"Did you hear what I told just you? You're in hot water here. I may have to call in the police officer."

Once more, there was the same response from him, only the smile was even larger. What the hell, I thought. In my experience most kids would be trembling by now, some even crying, but this kid just looked at me, the smile on his face growing larger as I increased the threats. I resisted the temptation to smack him for disrespect. I didn't yell at him. I stopped intimating about banishment to Alcatraz. I was the adult in the room or so I told myself. That was true, wasn't it?

"Listen kid," I tried to say calmly. "I'm about to give you a swat for what you did and your attitude. Do you understand me?"

Nothing. Only David's darn smile, now the size of a pumpkin. The smile was disconcerting, as was the increased twitching. The more I piled on the threats, the more David smiled and twitched. With a mind like a steel trap, I finally realized that something was wrong here. Was this disrespect or...? My intuition took over.

"David, I'm going to call your mother. Eventually, I reached her at work on the first ring and explained the entire situation.

"You don't understand," she said. "David reacts to stress by smiling. The greater the stress, the bigger the smile; he can't help it. It's weird, I know. If you wish to speak to the child psychologist who is treating him ..."

"That won't be necessary."

"Will he still receive a swat?"

"Not at this time. Let's get together for a parent conference tomorrow. In the meantime, let's figure out how to avoid false fire alarms. Together, we can determine an appropriate response."

"Thank you."

Turning to David, I said, "No swat today."

His smile faded a bit.

"No police today."

The twitching abated a bit."

"No capital punishment today."

An almost blank look appeared on David's face and all twitching stopped. I decided to let it go at that point. I always wondered what happened to David. Maybe he joined the CIA. Can you imagine David as a spy in the hands of the KGB? "Tell us everything or we will torture you!" The image is wonderful as he provides his captors with a big smile. Of course, David could also run for political office.

Three cases dealing with swats and three different responses by kids. You learn a lot in a Dean's Office, the serious stuff and the funny stuff. For example, there was Peter, who was sent to the Office for calling his teacher, and I quote, "an old bastard." Upon questioning, Peter denied the accusation, stating that his teacher was mistaken. What he had said was this: his teacher was an "old badger." Peter's retort was so forceful, if not quick, that he left me wondering. Bastard or badger, which was it? It was one of those cases, teacher's word against the student. Who was telling the truth?

"Peter, what is a badger?"

"Some kind of burrowing animal, I think."

"Pretty good. By the way, have you ever heard the song, *Fight on for Wisconsin?*"

"Sure, we lived in Madison before we moved to Los Angeles."

"Do you know another meaning for the word badger?"

"To bug someone?"

"How about to harass, or torment — to annoy someone."

"Badgers don't do that. They're just little guys with short legs, long claws, and a thick tail."

"What about kids? Do they ever badger their teachers?"

"Yeah, I guess so."

"Did you badger your teacher?"

"I guess I did."

"But you didn't call him an old b...?"

"Right."

Such is the life of a Dean. You're always trying to sort out the truth from all the lies. Bastard or badger, you can take your choice. Eventually, I sorted things out with Peter.

Yes, I knew a little about being a Dean. The middle school was a good teacher. There I slowly developed my personal techniques and uniquely appropriate strategies in dealing with the middle school criminal element. I learned enough to survive in the Deans Office; that was for sure.

Chapter 6

Empathy

"I've got a tough case coming in from Mrs. Lopez. Looks like he was trying to start a fight with a ninth-grader in her Art class. Imagine that kid's chutzpah, a seventh-grader taking on Mohammad Ai."

That was Mrs. Morrison, the Principal's secretary. Apparently, she was deputized to escort this pugnacious rascal to the Deans Office. Aware of my devious but deliberate Dean techniques, she said, "Going into your act now?"

I would have phrased my antics somewhat differently: middle school survival strategies. It went something like this:

First, before the belligerent kid came into the office, I dimmed the lights in the office as low as possible, darkening the room to the extent possible. It helps in reducing stimuli in the already over-stimulated kid, who is already overly upset (make that humiliated) at being kicked out of the classroom before all of his friends.

Second, speaking slowly and in almost a whisper, I asked the kid to please sit down. I resisted the temptation to jump right on the kid. Then I would pretend I was finishing some important work as I typed away on the computer. What was I typing always comes up? I was rewriting Tolstoy's *War and Peace* in English for the English Department (please don't believe that). What's the purpose of all this? Very simply, it gives the kid a chance to calm down. By the way, the strategy also works in the classroom in some sort of amended form.

Third, check the teacher's note. Really read it, especially the hidden stuff between the lines, such as emotions, frustrations, hidden agendas. Then ask the kid, "Do you know why the teacher referred you to the Dean's Office?" This helps to get everyone on the same page before talking about consequences. Expect to hear a sophisticated vibrant defense. "She's just mad at me." Or, "I didn't do it." The denial responses are limitless and occasionally quite creative.

Fourth, once you've decided what to do, inform the kid about what happens next. Do this in a quiet voice, always showing respect and concern for the kid. This is the Dean's Office, not a *Star Chamber*."

Fifth, where possible try to include the student in determining what should happen. That's not always easy, but can be very helpful. Suggest, if possible, a couple of options. Find out what he can buy into. Naturally, this is not always possible where certain incidents occur, such as fighting, drugs are involved, stealing, destroying school property, or threatening another student. And, of course, there is the time element. Can you do this before the next client clamors for your attention?

These strategies worked for me in the Deans Office and in the classroom, but, and I must admit this, not always at home with my own kids. There capital punishment often seemed the most valid option.

Perspective is also needed as a Dean. I learned that immediately. The Deans Office and the classroom are both in the "second chance business." We want to help students through tough times. We want to keep them in school. We want them to be productive and successful in their studies. We want all this even when they're fighting us. We're not into the punitive business, an occasional swat notwithstanding. And all this is helped by a large dose of empathy. You know, trying to understand the world from the student's perspective. I never had a problem with that, partially because I got into a few scrapes myself, not as a student, but as a teacher.

The Mummy

First, let me say I wasn't guilty. Good to have that out of the way. Second, I was a victim of circumstances. Now, as to what happened.

I was teaching a seventh-grade World History class with a lot of gifted and creative students. When studying Ancient Egypt and perhaps putting too much emphasis on "mummification," a charming young lady asked a most innocent question: "Dr. Livingston, can we make a mummy in class?" And before I could respond, another charmer said, "I've got a four-foot doll at home. We can use her." As I was gathering my thoughts, a boy stood and said, "My dad's a doctor and my mom is a nurse. We've got plenty of bandages around the house." Well, you can see where this is going. I gave into the oldest axiom in the universe: "Go with the Force." I capitulated with certain qualifications. We would really have to learn about mummification. That meant some serious research, even as we tackle the Greeks and Romans. The students agreed.

Three weeks later the class was ready. The room lights were turned off. Only three large candles provided light and the right atmosphere. The kids all wore robes, as did the teacher. I really did. The doll was placed on a long table. Incense was burned for authenticity. The three high priests, selected by the class, officiated while I watched. The class began chanting. Ointments were applied to the doll. Bandages soon followed. In time the doll was mummified. Ancient Egypt would have been proud.

At this point, you're asking, "Where did things go wrong?" It all began with an innocent query from a usually quiet student. "What should be done with the mummy?"

"I'm not sure. It really belongs to the class. You'll have to decide."
"It's up to us?"
"Yes, I think so."

After some discussion the students left the question open. They would make a decision the next day, or at least that's what they indicated. The mummy would remain in the room.

As I was signing in the next day, the Principal approached me, asking, "Did your students make a mummy yesterday?"

I knew the game. When the principal asked a question, he already knew the answer.

"Yes."
"Where is it now?"
"In my classroom."
"Oh?"

Again, the game... Oh, meant look out, something nasty is up.

"Come with me to my office."

We shuffled to his office. Inside seated at his desk was the mummy in question.

"Is that your mummy?"
"Yes, I think so, but with all the bandages it's tough to know."

My principal wasn't into levity.

"Why is it in my office?"
"I haven't the slightest."
"I want it removed by your class."
"Period 4."

As I was leaving the office, I couldn't resist asking, "It's a pretty sharp-looking mummy, isn't it?"

The principal glared at me and then the faintest of smiles appeared before he said "Passable."

Before I could respond, he said, "Out."

I did knowing that I still had job and my teaching credential was still intact. I also knew the Principal behind his gruff exterior was at least a little empathetic.

The Underground Newspaper

Again, let me reiterate, I'm not guilty. Once more, I was a victim of circumstances almost beyond my control. In this sense I'm a kind of a serial victim. It all began the year I finally got tenure, the Holy Grail of teachers. I could still be fired, but only after a protracted due legal process. Life in public education is always a little nicer with that security. Anyway, back to my next misadventure. It began with the Principal in an uproar.

"No one else will do it?"
"Why me?
"Process of elimination, Dr. Livingston."
"You mean I low man on the pole."
"Consider it a promotion."
"More money?"
"No."
"An extra conference period?"
"No."
"Well, what?"
"You'll be in my good graces."

I got his drift. It's always good to be on good terms with the Principal. Still, I resisted.

"I've never taught journalism."
"You read the paper."
"Yes."
"That's enough for me."
"I read it; I don't publish it."
"Mrs. Scanlon is having a baby. She's out. You're in."

And that's how I inherited for one year the Journalism Class. The class was largely made up of really bright ninth-graders, who could easily pass the State Graduation Test before matriculating to Cal Tech, Harvard, or USC. The kids were smart, creative, and full of initiative as they watched their older peers on college campuses in the mid 60's. They witnessed the civil rights movement, the feminist movement, the anti-war movement, and the beginning of the environmental movement. There were more movements than in a fine Swiss watch.

At first things went well. What did that mean? I got out of the way. The editors did their part. The reporters reported. The paper came out on time each month. The faculty liked it. Parents seemed please. What could go wrong? Well… It began with rebellion in the ranks; the editors were out for blood.

"That's it, Dr. Livingston. We're tired of it."
"And the 'it' is what?"
"The Principal's red pen."

I got it. Before any edition was published, it was submitted to the Principal for his approval. He could delete and did. He could alter and did so. Too often the submitted edition came back lit up like a Christmas tree.

"It's censorship."

"Well…"

"It's perversion of our journalist prerogatives."

"It's a school paper."

"It's suppression. Every time we're critical of school policy, slash goes the red pen."

"It's the principal's right."

"He deletes our editorials about student rights."

"He's got district authority."

"Those are Stalinist policies."

"What do you want?"

They told me.

"I can't have anything to do with this."

"We know."

"I could lose my job."

"We understand."

"I hope so."

A month later a newspaper appeared in every teacher's mailbox. Hundreds of copies were handed out to students at nutrition and lunch, most of which found their way home. Soon the school telephone was ringing off the ubiquitous hook: upset parents, unhappy downtown administrators, average citizens, each with a comment. Soon after I received a dreaded note from the Principal: "See me."

So I did.

"Did you know about this?" he asked while flourishing the paper before my innocent eyes.

"This particular edition?"

"This outrage!"

"No."

"You weren't aware your students were planning to publish this underground newspaper?"

"This exact edition, no."

"You never saw it?"

"Never until I was given a copy."

"Hard for me to believe."

"Hard for me, too."

"What?"

"Just agreeing with you, Sir."

That's the way it went for a time. Then things got sinister.

"I think you're trying to create a Berkeley situation here."

"Berkeley?"

"You know, that People's Park stuff. That agitator... That Mario Savio guy and the free speech movement... The anti-bra movement on campus... The 'get out of Vietnam' blabber...'

"These are middle school kids."

"Which you're training for Berkeley."

"Sir, I went to San Francisco State. Most of us couldn't afford to demonstrate for anything beyond our next meal."

"You're a provocateur."

"You ask me to be the journalism teacher against my wishes."

"A dreadful mistake."

"I agree."

We had reached an impasse.

"Do you know how this makes me look downtown?"

"No."

"I could have you fired."

"I have tenure. You just signed off on that."

"Terrible mistake. But I could still push."

"You could and I can make two phone calls."

"To whom?"

"The NEA and ACLU," I answered defiantly.

That ended our discussion. In time things blew over. Two things, however, were true. First, the kids had really published (at their own expense) a really fine paper which most of the faculty liked. I had, I must admit, intellectual empathy for them. Second, I had worn out my stay in the middle school. I had drained the administrative empathy tank. It was time for me to move on to a high school where I could get into more trouble.

Chapter 7

Viking Land

Though I don't like to consider myself a slow learner, it did take me six years to navigate my way from the middle school to James Monroe High School, where the students called themselves the "Vikings of the Valley." What President James Monroe and Nordic Vikings had in common, I never understood, and I'm a history teacher. Once there, I taught US History and US Government. I also gave some time to the Dean's Office at the invitation of the Vice-Principal, Larry Jenkins. There was no question about it, he was a straight arrow, a clean-as-a whistle guy, a no nonsense person, and a by-the-rules guy. You get the picture.

And for two periods a day, I was his personal messenger and enforcer with certain kinds of delicate problems. My work began in A-period. Time slot: 7:00 a.m. to 8:00 a.m. before school started. It was a time for command performance by me in a telephone booth size "head" for men. I know. A little explanation is needed.

It was the late "60's" — 1968 to be exact. The old USA was going up in smoke. War demonstrations, pro and con, about our involvement in Vietnam made the daily nightly news and a mess on the streets. There was rioting in Chicago where Mayor Daily, a "law and order" guy, turned his police loose on the demonstrators. Civil rights demonstrations, some peaceful, others not so, competed for airtime on the streets of

Birmingham and throughout the "Jim Crow South." It was the year of Martin Luther King was assasinated in Memphis and Bobby Kennedy was killed in Los Angeles. It was a time of student protest, bra burning, and drug induced joy in San Francisco's Height-Ashbury area. Not to be outdone, the People's Park in Berkley combined all these elements as part of the contemporary U.C. unofficial curriculum. Civil disobedience and student protests flooded into the nation's awareness.

My boss tried to stem the leak in the social dam. And I, unfortunately, was to be his human cork. He wasn't a bad guy. He just wanted a peaceful, predictable, law-abiding world in which civility reigned and rules were followed. Not much, you might think, to ask for in a time of social chaos. What did that mean in everyday school practice?

Concerning beards, long hair, and mustaches, the school policy was "nada." It was my job to work with the senior boys who silently protested almost everything by growing hair These young men violated our strict (possibly absurd) grooming standards. The "saints be preserved," they had grown beards and mustaches, and some even had long shoulder length hair. It was my job to trim this atrocious behavior.

It went something like this. I would meet with a young man in the office around 7:30 a.m. His parents were not invited to this meeting, but were aware of it. If he didn't show, they would be notified for parent conference. Let's assume the young man in question was John. I would take him across the hall to a Men's Faculty Bathroom, really a small cubical just large enough for two people if they stood rather uncomfortably close. Inside I would lock the door. There was no need for uninvited guests, nor was there room. As you might expect, John was not happy about this meeting. Truth be told, I wasn't overjoyed either.

Below the Belt, Incident #1

"John, we need to talk."

"So talk."
"Your beard."
"What about it?"
"It has to go."
"No way."
"You're not listening."
"No, you're not listening."

In situations like this, as you can see, I always got off to a good start with the hairy culprit. My powers of convincing were obviously at their peak.

"We need to really talk."
"You said that earlier."
"And you need to listen."
"B.S."
"Possibly, John, but you still need to."
"No way."
"I'm asking for five minutes of your time to avoid a suspension and keeping you from playing in tonight's football game."

It's always good to have some leverage on a client. John was a starting defensive end and he was pretty good. Some of the small local colleges were interested in him. His coach didn't mind John's beard as long as he raised hell on the opposing quarterback. Very pragmatic of the coach… At 6:2 and 215 pounds of muscle he was a big guy. In the confines of the restroom he was formidable and intimidating. I tried to keep my wits about me.

"This is intimidation."
"Probably."
"Five minutes?"
"Okay."

At this point I handed John a bladeless razor. I knew better than to take chances with a full Gillette.

"Here's the deal. I really don't care about your fuzzy beard. I don't give a damn about your mustache. But the school does. If you don't remove it, you won't play another game, attend the prom, or be in the graduation ceremony."
"Miss the prom?"
"Only good citizens attend."

At this point I took advantage of the poor guy.

"Look, I've seen you with that lovely young lady walking hand in hand across the quad. I assume you're taking her to the prom."
"I bought the tickets last week."
"Well, why jeopardize that. Just shave the facial stuff."
"That's crap."
"Perhaps, but it's also reality. That girl wants to go with you to the prom. Make it happen. And as to graduation…"
"Same cutthroat deal?"
"Yes."

At this point John became a lawyer.
"The guys in the Black schools can grow beards."
"That's true."
"Hispanics can."
"Only the guys."
"Why can't we?"

What could I say? "School rules." Talk about a dumb answer.

"This is a different school."
"Lousy rules."
"No argument there."
"I'm not going to do it."

We had reached that point. It always seemed to happen. It was so predictable. And heart of heart, I hated this moment. It was time for me to hit this kid below the belt and really hard.

"Lets talk about your parents."
"Why?"
"Graduation ceremony."
"So?"
"What happens during the ceremony?"
"We get our diplomas, yell a lot, and release balloons."
"And?"
"Go to Disneyland!"
"And what else?"
"I…"
"Your parents hold their breath for sixty seconds when they hear your name called. For one minute, they only see you walking from your seat on the football field to the rostrum. They see you shake hands with the Principal and receive your diploma. For those few seconds, they see their dreams come true. You've graduated."

"So?"
"So, why take it away from them? Why hurt them?"

Generally, that sealed the deal. Kids may fuss with their parents, but they really don't want to hurt them. Even so, it was always good to have a convincer.

"Let me tell you something. Unless it has already occurred, just before graduation, your Uncle Sam is going to send you a draft notice and, as healthy guy, you are going to pass your physical. In no time you'll exchange Levis and football pads for jungle green and your nice suburban room for a rather large barracks. Guess what happens next?"
"You tell me."

"You no longer practice in the stadium. You're practicing new drills in bootcamp as part of your infantry training. You're preparing for a different kind of game. Do you understand me?"

"Sort of."

"Not good enough. Here's the deal. Your next stop may be Vietnam. And once in Vietnam you can grow as much hair as you want. Nobody will give a rat's ass."

"So?"

"So this… If you get killed there, all your parents will have are memories, including your graduation. So tough guy, if you want to take this away from your folks, go ahead."

"This isn't fair."

"The world isn't fair, John. Get used to it. And by the way, put away your stubborn adolescent aghast. It's getting pretty old.

"I could be sent to Germany. The Cold War is still on."

"Yeah, you could be sent to Berlin, but that's not what happened to seven of our guys from this school. They never saw a pretty Fraulein. If you want to meet them, I'll take you over to the Westwood Military Cemetery. You can check a few of them out. No hurry. Those guys aren't going any place. If you are still pissed we'll drive over of the VA Hospital in Westwood.

"You're a piece of work, Dr. Livingston."

"Tell me about it."

That did it. Mortality and love mixed in a special way, even if they get together in a faculty head with emotions flowing hot and heavy.

As for me, I always had mixed feelings. I hated being a jerk about facial hair, but was relieved that a mom and dad's photo album would contain graduation photos. As I said, you learn a lot in the Deans Office, including being an S.O.B.

Hitting Below the Belt, Incident #2

I was involved in many parent conferences. They're never really enjoyable even if useful. Usually a parent has to take off work, or forego household responsibilities. Generally speaking, that's not a good thing. Usually there's only one reason for a conference. A son or daughter is in trouble. "What did he do this time?" is often asked. Almost always it's the mother who shows up. Assuming there's a dad at home, he's at work. If no father at home, the mother covers all bases. This is particularly hard on Hispanic moms and so often infuriating to me in the Dean's Office. I will explain.

"Good morning, Mrs. Torres. Thanks you for coming in. Jose, pull out that chair for your mother."
"Thank you."
"Do you know why I ask you for a parent conference?"
"Jose is in trouble."
"Yes. He's ditching school, failing his classes, and disrespecting his teachers.

My Spanish was scant, not a good thing in a school heavily populated by Hispanics. That being the case, I used an interpreter whenever possible. In this particular case, I had an unusual bright helper, a senior girl, Evelyn, who had been sent to the Dean's Office last year for disrespecting the teacher. After working things out, she requested me for Teacher Assistant position. I, of course, was delighted.

Prior to the parent conference with Mrs. Torres, I met with Evelyn.

"That's the deal. Mom speaks little English and I need you to interpret. Translate the words, but also the feelings. Do the same thing in reverse when I speak. And if you catch anything I should know, tell me. Okay?"
"Okay."

Evelyn translated my opening remarks. Mrs. Torres said she understood. After that I covered everything that was going on in school. A great sadness came over Jose's mother. In Spanish she responded. Evelyn translated.

"I tell Jose to listen to the teacher and do what she asks. I make his lunch before the sun is up and then leave to for work. I ask him to do his homework after school. I told him not to hang around with his gang friends. What else can I do?"

I watched Jose while his mother spoke. There was a slight hint of a smirk. Evelyn saw it too. It took all my control to avoid belting that kid into the middle of tomorrow. Instead, I asked…

"What kind of work do you do?"
"I work at the Hilton in Los Angeles. I clean rooms all day."
"Change the bedding?"
"Si."
"Clean the bathrooms?
"Everyday."
"Jose's dad?"
"He's in jail."
"I'm sorry."

What could I say? Mrs. Torres had been dealt a bad hand. I turned to Jose.

"Jose, let me get this straight. Your mother tells you all the right things to do, right?"
"So?"
"But you don't listen, correct?"
"So?"

One more "So" and I was going to kill this kid. Fortunately, Evelyn saved me, whispering to me, "He's a real smart ass. Don't lose your cool."

"Jose, your mother works hard to put food on the table and to provide you with a place to live. She cleans up somebody's mess every day. Why not help her? Stop hurting her."

Jose just stared at me, smirking even more, saying, "I'm not hurting her. She's just upset with me." Mrs. Torres was crying softly now, and I was closer to homicide. Evelyn looked like she wanted to kick this guy in the groin.

"You're not hurting your mother?"
"Si."
"One question, Jose."
"What?"
"See this paper weight. If I picked it up and you thought I was going to throw it at your mother, what would you do?"
"I'd stop you."
"Why?"
"Because you could hurt her."
"I don't get it. If you won't let me hurt your mother, why do you do it?
"I don't."
"Check your mother."

Mrs. Torres was sobbing. Evelyn gave her some tissue and embraced her. I just watched. Finally, I made some suggestions with Maria's help.

"Mrs. Torres, take Jose to work with you for a few days if the hotel will permit. Let him see how hard you work. I'll recommend that he be in a Continuation School and that our Career Office find some part-time job for him. If I had the power, I'd take him down to the

Navy recruiter. That might help him to grow up. For now just take him home."

Mrs. Torres thanked me. I watched the mother and son leave before I turned to Evelyn.

"Not sure I accomplished anything today. I tried to hit him below the belt, but …"
"You did okay, Dr. Livingston. You really did. Don't be too hard on yourself."

As always, what could I say? You win some and you lose some… Que sera sera…

Hitting Below the Belt, Incident #3

Javier Flores was a big kid and into gangs. Academically, he was floundering with D's with U's in cooperation. Much like the *Book-of-the-Month Club*, he got into a near fight each semester. Now that he was a senior in poor standing, the school wanted to ship him out. It was up to me to give him the bad news before the ubiquitous parent conference.

"Javier, that's the story."
"End of the line?"
"Unless you change your ways."
"It is the end of the line."
"Yes."

We just looked at each other. What else could we do? Javier didn't seem angry, just sort of philosophical about the whole thing. I just thought about the "end of the line." It was enough. I opened the bottom drawer to my desk and brought out three tiny toy trains. They were labeled A, B, and C. I placed them on the desk.

"Javier, I've shared my toy trains with a few students. Perhaps you would like to learn about them?"

Javier seemed nonplus by my question. Shamelessly, I went on.

"See Train A. It's headed toward UCLA. Train B is headed toward an occupational school or perhaps a community college. Train C is going off the track. Big crash is in its future, possibly even jail or death."

Javier just stared at the trains. He probably knew what was coming. He wasn't a dummy.

"Which train are you on, Javier? Which train would you like to be on?"
No answer. I waited. Finally Javier said, "That's below the belt."
"Choose anyway."
"Train B."
"Meaning?"
"I don't want to end up in jail or dead in the streets."
"There's a train ticket in your pocket. Use it."

Javier barely graduated and I didn't see him for many years. Then one day while attending a convention in the Air Tel Hotel, I heard a voice yelling, Dr. Livingston, is that you?" It was Javier. He was nicely dressed: sport coat, tie, nice slacks and polished shoes. He fast stepped over to me.

"You were a Dean?"
"Almost retired."
"Still got those trains?"
"I do."
"They saved my life."

Javier went on to tell me his story: he left the gang life behind him, went to Community College for his A.A. degree, and had a good job at the hotel. He was in charge of the car rental business and buses for large groups. He was married and had two kids. We talked more about a lot of things, but in the end I was left with one question. What was the magic in the toy train that worked with Javier? If I could capture and bottle it, life in the Deans Office would be so much easier.

Chapter 8

Getting to Know The Job

My first day on the job... Mr. Mendoza, bless his bureaucratic heart, issued me my basic equipment. Item #1 - a brick-like radio that clipped to my belt was his first offering, along with a code list. Compared to later credit card size cell phones, my "brick" felt like a giant anchor, especially when I was moving fast (which was not too often) or trying to stop a fight between two husky guys (which the job required). Clipped to my belt was the way Mr. Mendoza phrased it; I preferred lugged by my body. A slight difference in opinion, you suggest. Tell that to my right hip.

"Don't lose your phone."
"Why would I do that?"
"It happens, especially when you're breaking up a fight."
"Can I use the phone as a weapon? You know, knock the kid over the head with it."
"No."
"Doesn't seem fair."

Paying no attention to my comments, Mr. Mendoza continued. "Don't shout on the radio. Keep your voice calm and low."
"I can do that."
"You better. And another thing, use the code."
"10-4."

"Pretty good. Know anything else?"
"10-9"
"I'm not going to repeat my question."
"10-4."

Changing the subject, Mr. Mendoza said, "Here are your keys, five of them."
"Five?"
"One is for your office door. The second one is for the file cabinets. Lock the door and cabinets before leaving school. The third one is to the buildings, all of them. The fourth one opens all the gate locks. The last one will get you into the Custodians Office in an emergency. Don't lose the keys."
"10-4."
"Any questions?"
"Just one. Did the school ever consider a universal key; you know, one that fits all locks."

Mr. Mendoza let that one pass. As to my new weighty equipment, I was thankful the school didn't have a swimming pool. Saving an exhausted swimmer about to go down for the third time was not an appealing thought for a person still learning the dog paddle and weighted down with bricks and keys.

"Anything else," I asked.
"The office secretary will give you an access code to your computer. Memorize it. Don't write it down."
"Youthful eyes?"
"Exactly."

Mr. Mendoza then surprised me. "Look, a couple of things. First, you're the first faculty elected Dean. Every past Dean was appointed by the Principal and he doesn't like the new system."
"Do you?"
"Not really."

"Fair enough."

"Jenks has his concerns, too, as does Officer Rio. We're a small club. We need to count on each other. We need to be in agreement. Sometimes we even need to keep secrets. Can you keep secrets?"

"Unless the parents are using sodium pentothal, yes."

"I'll let that pass. The appointment system gave us the kind of people we needed. With an election, we're unsure. You're a new commodity, kind of a surprise for us. A sort of experiment... The guys are a little nervous. You understand?"

"I'm not one of the old boys."

"Exactly."

"Even though I'm the oldest one around here?"

"Even though... Any problems with this?"

"Not really."

"Good. I've told the Jenks and Rio to help you out."

"I appreciate that.

Jenks caught up with me a little later. As promised, he was helpful.

"Here's a list of phone numbers, about twenty. Check them out later. Before the semester is over, you'll probably use all of them.'

"Right."

"Add new ones as necessary. Got it?"

"Got it."

"Here's a map of the school, including all the fire alarms, and gates. Each one is numbered. Your supervision in the morning will be gate 5, which is next to the Adult School. At noon, you supervise in the quad. At lunch, the same, plus the athletic fields, where the smokers hang out. After school, gate 7, the student parking lot. During periods 1 through 6 you are in the Office unless something happens. Questions?"

"When do we eat?"

"On the run and during the last minutes of period 4 just before the lunch bell."

That was it. Weighted down with keys and a phone, I would also starve to death. At that moment, I decided to have a food drawer in the desk, and a portable refrigerator, if possible, to back up my sack lunch.

Before leaving me, Jenks said, "You'll be O.K. I'll help you. I'm not as bad as I seem."
"Worse?"
"Sometimes."
"Thanks for the warning."
"You're welcome."

And so began my first day as the new Dean... Somewhat wet-behind-the-ears, I headed to Gate 5 to supervise the morning traffic.

Gate 5

This cyclone steel gray gate was sandwiched between the Adult School and some temporary bungalows used to house our overpopulated student body. The gate faced out onto a busy street fronting the school. My job was simple. Deter non-VNHS students from entering. Watch for suspect vehicles cruising the street. Assist parents, who were looking for the Main Office. And finally, at 8:10 a.m. precisely, close and lock the gate before patrolling the hallways for tardy students.

"Boring," I thought aloud to myself.

I needed to jazz up this gate deal. I couldn't just stand there, sentry-like, stoic and silent. I quickly determined what I would do to keep myself awake. Very simply, I would say something to each student entering school. In time I developed a complete repertory.

"Good morning."
"Hi."
"Have a great day."
"Nice jacket."

"Beautiful day."
"Looks like rain."
"Feeling O.K.?"
"Haven't seen you for a few days."
"Shortened day today."
"It's Friday, last day of the week."
"Don't be late."
"That backpack looks heavy."
"How did he Dodgers do?"
"Don't forget the game tonight."

At first, the words floated in the air before disappearing into a void known only to missing socks and loose change. Nothing happened. There was no response from the students. In retrospect, I can see why. Here was an unknown senior citizen speaking to them. Who the heck was he? Except for the students who had been in my classes, I was a mystery to most kids. I hadn't been introduced to the student body in any formal manner. I was just another face, another adult at the gate.

And then it happened, about a week later. My non-entity status changed.

"Enjoy your day."
"Thanks."

Someone had actually spoken to me.

"Do well on your test today."
"I need to."

Two people had talked to me. I was on a roll.

"Great haircut."
"Thanks for noticing."

It took about five weeks before a majority of the students were responding to my patter. Over the ensuing years, it got to the point where, if I didn't say anything, the kids would ask me if I were O.K. It doesn't get much better than that, especially when about 500 students entered through my gate each day.

The gate, I might add, no longer belonged to the school. My territorial imperative was in full bloom. This was my gate. My scent was on it.

Boredom ceased in the A.M. Now I had to figure out what to do in the afternoon at my other gate.

Gate 7

This gate overlooked a side street bordered by a large student parking lot on one side, and a series of small apartment houses on the other. Unlike the morning gate, there was plenty of activity here.

The last school bell ended the day and kick-started a mini Le Mans at my gate. Students rushed from classes, then to lockers, and finally headlong into the parking lot. Nobody wanted to be the last car out. Consequently, there was a mad rush to rev up engines and floor the gas pedal in the restricted confines of the parking lot. Those kids were good. Somehow they maneuver safely, obliged each other to avoid crashes, and exited the lot in fifteen minutes or less.

My job was to stay alive while controlling this mass of metal and humanity, and to watch out for gang-related problems of any sort. It was an action location. Still, I decided to 10-9 myself. New messages, though, were needed. As the cars reached the exit gate, I engaged.

"Hope you had a good day."
"See you tomorrow."
"Great looking car."

"Drive carefully."

"Keep it under 120."

"You're back rear tire needs air."

"Watch out for the walkers."

"What a paint job."

You guessed it. At first, the cars whipped out oblivious to my comments. Then slowly, the miracle happened again.

"Hope you had a good day."

"You, too."

"Stay safe."

"Same."

And so it went. Foot traffic in the morning,.. Hot sedans and pickup trucks in the afternoon… My world was complete. I was connecting with the student body, but not necessarily my colleagues.

"How did go at the gate," Rio asked.

"Easy street."

"You sure talk a lot to the students. Be careful, that could detract you from a serious problem."

"True."

"What'd you say to those kids?"

"Hi."

"That's it?"

"Sort of."

There was no way I was going to share my proprietary comments.

Jenks got into this, too, saying "I shouldn't get too friendly with the students."

"Just being neighborly."

"We need to keep our distance. We're law enforcement."

"Not much distance when they walk or drive right by me."

"They need to respect us."
"Agreed, but I don't see the connection."
"They need to fear us."
"I thought we just wanted them to be cool."
"You're impossible."
"But not hopeless."

Inspired by my communication skills, I decided to apply them to my nutrition and lunch supervision duties.

The Quad

During nutrition and lunch breaks, I prowled the blackish asphalt with a watchful eye, always looking for that fight about to break out, or the lonely backpack about to flee under new ownership. My job included keeping the campus clean — that is, garbage in the containers, not on *Mother Earth*. In addition to all this, I was expected to watch for smokers (whether cigarettes or pot) hiding in building nooks, or behind the football stands. Checking the heads for questionable behavior also claimed my attention. All in all, these responsibilities made the breaks go by fast. Would there be time to strike up a conversation, or at least break the verbal ice? I wondered and experimented.

"That looks like a great sandwich."
"How's the cafeteria food today?"
"You girls found a great spot on the grass."
"Nice music."
"Studying now! You must have a big test next period."
"Watch your purse, young lady. Wouldn't want to see it grow legs."
"Thanks for picking up your lunch bags."
"You'll need an umbrella tomorrow."

In time, a nod, or hand gesture said it all. My message was simple: "I'm around in case there is trouble. I'm your friend. You can count on me."

Over the years, that message took hold as I was getting to know the students at VNHS. The dividends would come in time. A lot of things happen in the quad. A repository of student good will helped everyone to survive. Two examples highlight this view

The Armenian Fight

I was on the quad at lunch minding my own business (and everyone else's) when it happened. Suddenly, as if pulled by a serious magnet, kids were walking fast, then loping, and then running all out toward the ROTC bungalow. Now kids only run for a couple of reasons. If the local radio station is handing out CD's, they'll run. If summer vacation beckons, they'll run. If a fight is taking place, they'll run to it unless they hear gunfire. They maybe primitive, but they're not stupid.

I grabbed my brick and alerted others of the possibility of a fight and then charged into the torrent of heaving human bodies. Before any other adult, I got to the fight, where an almost perfect circle had formed around the thrashing bodies of two very large male Armenians. Next to them was one kid, who, acting as a sort of referee, was trying to give the combatants room to fight. A cursory look indicated no knives, baseball bats, or *AK47's*. I could handle this one. I also realized I knew both of the guys. God was good. I bent over the struggling and perspiring giants and whispered.

"Hi guys, it's me, Dr. Livingston." There was no response beyond more grunts and groans. "Perhaps I could have your attention." Again, nothing audible… There was just a lot rolling, punching, and shoving at ground level. "I really need to speak to you guys." Nothing. Undeterred, I continued. "OK, here's the deal. I'm going to get up and walk toward the Administration Building. I want you to do the same. Let's not embarrass each other. Let's do this before things really get out of control."

True to my promise, I got up and slowly walked away from my battling, belligerent boys, and would you believe it, they got up and followed much to the dismay of the onlookers who wanted blood. Once we got to my office, I gave each a towel (for just such times), some cold water (from my mini frig) before we got down to business.

"First, let me say I'm glad you guys listened to me."

"No problem," Art, the taller of the two, said.

"Yeah, thanks for showing up" the other said. His name was Artie. "Thanks for breaking up our quarrel. We couldn't while everyone was looking. You known, the pride thing."

"My pleasure. Now what was this about?"

Dumb question. It was answered in repaid succession in Armenian, English, and words and phrases akin to Russian slang; it was something about a girlfriend and what others were saying, "He did that, She did this. The Slavic rumor mill was working overtime.

"Enough. I get the picture — unhappiness in the land of romance.

"He's ... Artie started to say.

"That's a lie," Art challenged back.

"Perhaps I should call the girl into the office to straighten things out. And along with her, all your parents, and the Soviet Secret Police."

Parents, that's a magic word in the Dean's Office. Most students dread the thought of parents in school.

"Any other way? Art asked.

"Yes."

"What?" Artie beseeched.

"Option #73."

"What's that?" was their coordinated response.

Of course, there was no Option #73. I just made it up. But it had a ring to it. It sounded pretty good, even to me.

"Works like this. I suspend you. We have a parent conference. You each sign a contract, no more fighting. Break the contract, move to a new school, different schools. One of you goes to school in the Falkland Islands, the other in New Guinea."

Fortunately, America students are geography-deficient. From the looks on their faces, they wanted to know how far apart these schools were in Los Angeles. These guys needed to watch the Discovery Channel.

"Suspension? Is that necessary? Art questioned.
"Special suspension, Option #73.5 for cases like this."
"Special ..." they both said in unison.
"You guys cooperated with me. I'll give you in-house suspension rather than the usual three days at home. You'll only miss two periods of school, periods 5 and 6 today, and I'll meet with your parents before school tomorrow."
"Thanks," they both uttered, relieved that their punishment wasn't worse."
"Right. You're receiving this dispensation because you cooperated with me. (which meant they didn't slug me). Your records are clean and your grades are okay. Let's keep it that way.
And that's what we did. But here's the salient point. Every day for almost a year I had said good morning to these chaps as they entered school through my gate. We knew each other. There was a relationship. And it stood up to the survival test when I asked them to follow me to the office. A dividend paid off.

Pregnancy on the Quad

Liz was always getting into scrapes. She was an out-of-control 10th-grader with a loud mouth and a penchant for acting stupid. She was also

pregnant and acting out her emotional life in school; that is, on the quad
all too often. I knew about her condition because she had requested a
transfer to a special school, McAlister High, where moms-to-be could
finish their course work and also receive prenatal care. Subject to parent
approval, a Dean had to approve such a transfer. I approved and Liz
thanked me by getting into two fights before she left.

"Why are you doing this, Liz? I asked after the second altercation.
"I was angry."
"You can't be fighting in your condition. You could hurt yourself."
"I was beating that bitch."
"Perhaps, but what about the baby. Something might happen."
"I'd kill the bitch."
"This isn't going well, Liz. How about giving me a break?'
"I didn't hit you."
"True enough, at least not on purpose."
"That was a mistake. I didn't see you. I wouldn't have thrown a
punch at you. Do you believe me?"
"Yes, I think I do."

Here's the thing for the uninitiated, Usually boys want you to break
the fight. Not so with girls. Guys accept a white flag. Ladies burn it.
With young men, you can grab them almost everywhere. With young
women it isn't that easy. My usual well-tested ploy was to grab a girl
around the stomach from behind with one arm while I stiff-armed the
other girl until the Marines arrived. That meant pulling hard on the
stomach. Not a good thing for a fetus.

"I never thought about that."
"Well, do so, Liz."
"What's going to happen?"
Your transfer came through. You leave in two weeks."
"Two weeks!"

"No opening until then. But don't worry I'm suspending you now. After you leave here today, you're not coming back. No more fights at Van Nuys."

"I won't be able to say goodbye to my friends."

"Call them on the phone. I can't take a chance on another fight."

"It's not fair."

"Tell that to the baby you're carrying."

"What do you mean?"

What did I mean? Each year I saw about 20 or more pregnant girls. Usually they were young 9th and 10th-graders who were doing poorly in their classes and exhibiting un-cooperative behavior in school. Almost always, the parents (most often the mom again) didn't know what to do with them. And the truth was, I didn't know either. With little exception, they didn't want to the boy (or man) involved and were going to seek county assistance once the baby was born. This new "love object" would be cared for by the family.

"Liz, think about it. You're failing your classes, fighting with other students, and pregnant. You won't let someone adopt your child, not even a deserving family with financial stability. You told me that last time we talked. What are we left with? You want your family and the taxpayer to take care of you. That doesn't sound very fair to me or to your kid."

"You're awful."

"What's awful is the future awaiting your kid. Every statistic, all the research about single moms in your condition suggests trouble: gangs, drugs, violence, and jail."

"It won't happen to my kid."

"Hopefully not, but the statistics are against you."

"I'm out of here."

"That's correct."

Liz got up and headed for the door. She stopped abruptly, turned, and said, "Thanks for saying something nice to me each day when I came to school. It helped.

"You're welcome."

Not a nice picture. The real world doesn't stop at the school door and sometimes it plays itself out on the quad in a most unusual way.

The Bloody Nose

I often wondered how a bloody nose on the quad at lunch helped me win an election. Even now, I'm still amused by what happened.

I was running for reelection as Dean and my usual critics were out in force. "You're too old for the job," was their general refrain. "The kids like you too much, which means you're not tough enough on them," was the added charge. "You don't support teachers enough. You're always taking the student side," was the final, devastating accusation leveled at me.

Answering these charges was not easy. I was older than most Deans, but not "old, old." I could still put on a burst of speed when necessary, at least for 100 yards. OK, reduce that to 50 yards. Anyway, speed is an overdone commodity with locked gates and fences around the school. Beyond that, sitting at my desk used little energy. The new office computer required cognitive skills, not muscular arms. In no way did I think of myself as a *Medicare Dean*.

As to toughness, that was always in the eye of the beholder. True I didn't yell often, lose my temper (unless part of an act), or show off for the faculty with very public demonstrations of my prowess. I just did my job, perhaps a little too quietly. If statistics meant anything, I suspended my fair share, arrested those needing incarceration therapy, and held numerous parent conferences where necessary. But perceptions are almost everything, and I didn't look and act tough enough. This was going to be an extremely tight election.

The last accusation did hurt. I always supported the classroom teacher and tried to uphold and protect the instructional program from the "tyranny of a few" jerks. I also always listened patiently to the student's side, which was different from taking the student's side. But what can one do when teachers talk at the lunch table?

"Livingston only suspended the kid for one day."
"I would have thrown the kid out of the school."
"He actually wants me to meet with the parents to explain how the kid disrespects me. Can you imagine that?"
"He didn't get to the four students I sent him just before nutrition. What's he doing in that office?"

And so it went. Of course, I had my supporters, but a tough election was still in the cards. It was just one week before the election of new Deans when it happened.

I was on the quad at nutrition talking to a charming senior, who was heading for Stanford when I noticed her eyes. They had grown in size. Realizing that I wasn't that appealing, I turned to see what had captured her retinas. Less than twenty yards away two students were going at it just outside of the Teacher's Cafeteria. Fists flying, blood flowing, and curses erupting, this was the real thing. I called it in and tucked my "brick" securely in my pants, and then dove into the melee, grabbing the bigger kid by his chest, leaving us face to face.

"Stop it." Nothing. "Knock it off." "Nothing. "Break it up." Nothing. By accident, not intent, the kid whacked me, then, realizing who had slugged, he said, "Sorry, Dr. Livingston!"
"Apologies accepted.

It was only then that I recognized the kid beyond the bloody mask as a student with a tardiness problem. He lived nearby and went home at lunch to check on his old sister who was ill. Getting back on time was the challenge. I had made a concerted effort to resolve the problem. I had almost adopted him (well, at least in school).

After some effort and the arrival of a teacher, the two guys were finally separated. It was then that I noticed blood all over me, as well as my charge. His nose was a full-blown *Old Faithful*, and it was spraying both of us.

"I gave him my much used wad of tissue, saying, "Pinch your nose. Let's get to the Nurse's Office fast. And at that precise moment, the bell to end lunch clanged, and faculty members poured out of the cafeteria. What's a guy to do, especially if he's in a tight election? The gods had provided me with an unimpeachable election ploy.

"Take it easy buddy. Keep pinching, but let's walk slowly. I don't want you to get dizzy."

You know what happened. The teachers walked by us and saw a true but somewhat staged scene. There I was, an old guy, covered in blood, grasping a rather large youth in a manly grip. As I said, perceptions can be everything. That beautiful, bloody nose proved fortuitous. It was worth at least 50 votes and victory. I almost didn't have the heart to suspend the kid. Almost... What I really wanted to do was give his reddened schnozzle a big kiss. Well almost ... And that's, God help us, is how a Dean survives in the quad.

Chapter 9

Gangs

"Here."

I was in my office, thirteen weeks into my new life as a Dean. Jenks was holding a small brown-colored package. As always, he was dressed in ironed Levis and a starched, crisp sports shirt, which looked great on his thirty something frame. A surfer, runner, and swimmer, Jenks was without question the athlete of the office. With a few years on him, I could match the starched part, but that was about all.

"What?"
"This just arrived. Here."
"What's this?"
"Certification."
"Really?"

I reached out tentatively for the package. I had been around Jenks enough to know he was given to tricks, jokes, and unusual surprises most often at someone else's expense. I carefully checked out the package.

"Doesn't seem to be ticking."
"Your lucky day."

Taking no chances, I held the package up to the light. I could discern no electrical wiring, or smell any toxic material.

"You're a trusting soul."
"Aren't, I."

Still unsure of what might be inside, I gingerly unwrapped the mysterious package. I noticed that Jenks had moved away from to a far corner of the office. Was he getting out of the field of fire? Was something about to go "bang?"

"Don't you want to see what it is?" I asked.
"I know what it is."
"Perhaps you would like to stand closer?"
"I'm fine here."

It was then that I noticed Jenks fidgeting with his *Polaroid* camera. What was he up to?

"Camera not working?" I questioned in my most subtle manner.
"Something jammed."
"Want some help?"
"No."

It was "do or die" time. Taking a deep breath, I closed my eyes and unwrapped the last folds of paper. Peeking out, I was surprised to find a glistening nameplate with stark black letters edged on a golden colored background — *Dr. Robert Livingston, Dean*. It was cool looking, and I must admit I was very impressed by my new tag, and the wooden stand, which came with it. I looked up at Jenks just in time to catch the *Polaroid* flash.

"You're official now," Jenks said with a large contagious smile. "What'd think, Mr. Dean?"
"Nice."
"Your desk is no longer nameless."

"True."
"Now the kids won't have to ask your name"
"Works with parents, too."
"It does."

I carefully arranged the plate on its wooden frame before placing both on my desk. I had to admit I felt more official. "Thanks."

"You've earned it. Three months without a major disaster."
"Not even a minor one."
"Even Rio is getting used to you."
"Now that is a breakthrough."

As I looked upon my nameplate with a certain pride, Jenks brought out another small parcel. "Here."

This was getting to be like Christmas, which didn't offend my marginal Jewish background at all.

"Another gift."
"Open it."
"No, I think I'll wait until Santa slides down the chimney."
"Open it!"
"Hold your horses."

I took pity on Jenks and stopped teasing him. I opened the package. Inside was a package of 500 office cards identifying me as a Dean at Van Nuys High along with a school address and phone number. No longer would I have to scratch this information out for those in need of the info.

"I like the black print on the white background."
"And the district logo?"
"And that, too."
"Well, you're almost fully prepared."

Fully prepared… What did he mean? What did he have up his sleeve? As I considered these questions, Rio came in with two of our beautiful student service workers, each picked personally by Jenks and both in love with his dashing frame. Each girl carried a large box.

"At last," said Rio.
"Finally." the girls echoed.
"Finally what?" I asked.
"Finally this," Jenks said with a twinkle in his eye.

With that, the boxes were placed on my desk with the command to open them now. I obeyed. I was no longer worried about a ticking cartoon bomb going off next to *Bugs*, at least not with everyone crowded into the office. The first box contained a pair of Levis, blue in color, and in my correct size. The second box presented me with a new pair of walking boots and two pair of white athletic socks. I was speechless … Well, almost speechless.

"This is too much."
"Your *Brooks Brothers* image needed changing," Rio clamored.
"You're like a mannequin on duty," one of the young ladies explained with a big smile.
"We were afraid you would choke to death with the way you cinch your tie," her fellow student assistant added.
"Cinched is an unusual word," I remarked.
"I work with horses," she replied.
"And Deans," Rio reminded me.
"There must be a difference," I suggested.
"Horses don't need office cards," Jenks retorted.

Truthfully, I was overwhelmed. Obviously some time and attention had gone into all this.

"Thanks everyone."
"Your wardrobe needed updating," Rio explained.

"Rio is being kind," Jenks added.

"Once more, thanks."

"We're making Friday informal dress day. Guess what you must wear on Friday?" Rio asked in his most intimidating voice.

"Levis and boots?"

"And a shirt," one young lady said with a hearty laugh.

"And a shirt."

"A colorful shirt," the other service worker reminded me. "Beige is out."

"Colorful?"

"Very," she said.

"Deal."

"Time for pictures," Jenks stated matter-of-factly.

On cue, everyone gathered around me and my gifts while Jenks clicked away after demanding smiles and no gang gestures. Again, as if on cue, everyone departed leaving me alone with my Jenks.

"One thing," I muttered.

"What"

"How do you know my size?"

"State secret."

"You won't tell. Doesn't matter. You must have talked to my wife."

"You're quick on the uptake."

"Well, thanks anyway. Be assured, I'll be dressed appropriately on Friday."

"We can't wait."

"What's on the agenda today?"

Smiling, Jenks said," Are you ready for your snap lesson?"

"Let's do it."

Snap lesson... That was Jenks' way of giving me a quick update on some aspect of the job. Today's topic was graffiti." With that Jenks handed me three items, a large photo book, a Polaroid camera, and a paintbrush. Believe it or not, I knew what Jenks had in mind.

"When we find graffiti on school property, especially the walls, we first photograph. Next we paint over it a soon as possible. The custodians have our own little supply of matching paint. Finally, we check our photo book to identify the artist. The trick was to remove the graffiti before the kids saw it and the artist (and his group) gains notoriety. We had done this in the middle school. I didn't mention that to Jenks.

Gang Relations

Jenks was lecturing. "Each year at the beginning of the fall semester, we meet with the seniors in BVN to continue an agreement. Basically, we ask for their assistance in helping us with the BVN freshman class to keep those kids out of trouble. 'Wanna be' tough guys can be a problem. Next, we maintain the status quo. Nothing goes down on campus. Keep the problems at least three blocks away from the school. Lastly, no problems on campus; lets keep the school safe for everyone."

"Kind of like a arms treaty with the Russians."

"Whatever."

"Has it worked, Jenks?"

"Reasonably well."

"Sounds good to me."

"Glad to hear it because you are designated to meet with the BVN seniors."

"Why me?"

"They asked for you."

"What?"

"You have earned their trust."

Squatters Rights

"I see you've been spending some time with the guys."

"Right, at nutrition and lunch, Jenks."

"How's it going?"
"Hard to tell."

Everyday I walked over to the "guys," the area where BVN members congregated at a long cement bench during nutrition and lunch. They never sat on it. They stood in front of it, lords of their kingdom wearing the uniform of the day — brown pants, white tee shirt, white socks, and black shoes. As a group, the ten or more husky gang-types with mainly baldheads made for a formidable spectacle. Though they held no deed to the property, no other students competed for the space. There was an unofficial understanding. This was BVN turf. No one challenged them.

As part of my supervision duties, I would saunter over to the bench adorned in my pressed blue suit and red power tie riveted against my starchy white shirt to make small talk. I remember the first time I did this.

"Morning, gentlemen." There was absolutely no response. "Nice day." Still no reaction… "I'm the new Dean." Deep grunts, nothing more. "If I can be of assistance, let me know." Silence. "See you later. Got to check out some fire alarms." Shrugs.

Each day I came back to the same welcome. It was the gate deal all over again until one nutrition …

"Hot out day."
"Yeah."
"What? You spoke?

I looked around. Someone had broken the ice. Who was it? Unexpressive faces refused to give away the speaker.

"Is this the beginning of a wonderful relationship?" I asked in my best *Bogart* voice.
"Something," an anonymous voice said.

Another voice. I was making progress, one utterance at a time. "Good to know you guys can speak," I said with a big smile. "I was beginning to worry about you."

"No need."
"O.K."

Jenks recalled that day now. "Do you know why they finally spoke to you yesterday?"
"Desperation?"
"Luis Martinez."
"What?"
"You remember him."

Luis Martinez

I did. Luis Martinez had been in a fight a week ago with a new kid from another school. It was difficult to determine who started the fight or exactly why. A few blows were thrown, along with a heavy dose of bad language and scary threats. Mr. Mendoza asked me to deal with the combatants. I did."

"If you guys continue this, either on or off campus, you will force me to transfer you to different schools. If your friends get involved, again, on or off campus, transfers will occur. I hope I've made myself clear."

During each subsequent parent conference, which was at different times, I explained the situation. Predictably, all parents nodded politely and gave me heartfelt looks. Both fighters submitted grudgingly to what I had said. "You'll need to sign this." I handed each family a statement explaining what had happened and what I had just said. It was co-signed by all. Then, to reinforce the seriousness of the situation, I requested Rio to step into the office. Together we went into a developing finely crafted script. I introduced Luis and his mother and explained the situation.

Rio responded with a mix of street Spanish, stern looks, and forceful hand gestures. He was impressive. It all added up to this.

"Luis, another fight and I may have to arrest you. Got it?"
"Yes."
"Louder!"
"YES!"
"That's better."

Having done his part, Rio departed with an official flourish. I now completed the job. Before Luis' mom left and he was readmitted to school, I changed the subject. "Luis, I've checked your grades. You're not doing very well." Students expected the Dean to focus on behavior, not their academic work. "In fact, if things don't improve, you won't graduate." As expected, his parents were in despair.

"He must."
"He should. But does Luis want to?"
"Do you?" Luis' father asked him. "Do you, Luis?"

He didn't answer his father's question. He checked out the office ceiling, my desk, the picture window, everything but his father.

"Luis, your dad asked you a question."
"Yeah, I want to graduate."
"Your grades don't indicate that."
"Luis, your younger brothers look up to you. "If you don't graduate, they may not."

It was my turn to bring the meeting to an end. I had to say something to his Luis' parents to give them hope and the boy a chance to survive.

"Luis, everything is up to you."

"Luis told his BVN buddies about the meeting."

"Really?"

"You were respectful and fair."

"Tell that to my kids at home."

"They're calling you the 'quiet dean' because you don't raise your voice."

"No kidding?"

"They should hear you in the office. You talk our ears off."

"But I don't yell."

"True enough."

"It's nice to be loved."

"Regardless, just watch your step with these guys."

"Reality check… I know they're capable of anything. I'm just trying to make school a place where they will be capable students. These guys are anything but dumb."

Changing the subject, Jenks said, "Time for a little history."

"Fine by me."

With that, Jenks explained a few things to me about BVN. "This gang is one of the oldest in the Valley."

"How old?"

"Over 40-years. It began on Delano Street, on of the original barrios. Some people say it started as *Pacheco Club* and that its members were involved in the *Zoot Suit Riots* during the war."

"No way."

"There are grandfathers out there who attended here and were dues paying members of BVN."

"Jesus."

"We've got school books dating back to the 70's, which have BVN graffiti in them."

"That's a lot of creative writing."

At that moment, Rio came in with a rush. With his pronounced stomach, protective vest, dark blue uniform, gun belt, and a monstrous inhaling of air, he resembled an M-1 tank dashing across the North African deserts.

"Another tagger tagged. In the hands of his probation officer now... Good work Doc. You really nailed this artist."

Doc! A fondness in the voice... A bit of merit given... I was in Dean heaven.

"Glad I could help."
"Don't get full of yourself. It's a long semester."
"Me?"
"You."

Over the passing years, I had a number of special moments with BVN as my tenure (make that legacy) settled in at Van Nuys High.

Breakfast

In time I pushed and nudged the guys to improve their grades. Generally, my efforts fell short. Underachieving was a habitual pattern for them and a constant thorn in my side. Almost always, it led to kids dropping out of school. One day, perhaps out of desperation, certainly not in a sane moment, I made a foolhardy promise to the group.

"Here's the deal. I buy breakfast at *I-Hop* to anyone who has C's or better and no U's."
"That's tough. What about at only one D?"
"O.K., Joaquin, I compromise on that."
"No U's is too hard. Some of these teachers give me a U the first time they see me."
"Miguel, what would you suggest?"
"Get rid of the teacher."
"Besides that?"
"No more than two 'U's."

"Can you live with that, Carlos?"

"If you can…"

"I can."

So we did it. I checked their mid-term report cards. Out of about twenty guys, five qualified. A week later, at 7:00 a.m. exactly, we settled into our seats at the local *International Pancake House*, one graying older man with five glistening baldies. What a sight we must have made.

Concerned for my wallet, I said, "Try the special. Lots of good choices there." My troop, however, had something else in mind.

To a man, they each ordered a large orange juice, a stack of big pancakes, three eggs, slab of bacon, extra toast, and hot chocolate. They showed no mercy. My wallet was taking a real beating.

This was the typical order. If these guys were anything but dumb, they were also anything but shy in ordering. They knew a good thing when they saw it. When the waitress looked at me, I simply said, "An aspirin and the bill, and the darkest, strongest coffee you have." As to the five young men, they attacked their food with relish and good manners, interesting breakfast talk, and a nice "thank you" to the waitress. They also checked to see what kind of tip I would leave. Needing to impress them, I dropped two fives.

A year later, having learned a few financial lessons, I made another deal for the same grade improvement. I would cook breakfast for them in the Home Economics room.

"You'll cook?" was the disbelieving response."

"I know how to cook."

"Like at *I-Hop?*"

"Better."

"This we have to see."

The deal was struck. Eight weeks later I had seven budding scholars. I then set things in motion.

Once she recovered from her shock, the Home Economics teacher granted me permission to use her immaculate kitchen.

"You're buying the food?"
"Yes."
"You're cleaning up?"
"You won't know we had been there."
"No food fights."
"Just breakfast."
"Out by first period?"
"Of course."
"God help you. Do you need anything?"
"A good cookbook?"

The day was scheduled. Mr. Mendoza was alerted. Jenks and Rio, Protestant and Catholic by upraising, said prayers on my behalf. Unknown to my guests, I enlisted the help of their girl friends. Joining me were four girls, who volunteered to help me cook breakfast. Talk about covering your stomach. The great day came and everything went off without a hitch. I was now solidly an ad hoc member of BVN. Even the cooking teacher was impressed.

The Tour

It was in my third year that I made the fateful decision. I would take 20 members of BVN on a tour of our local community college. This had never been done before at our school. It was like Lewis and Clark stepping out into the unknown once they left St. Louis. I still remember Jenks' face when I suggested the tour.

"Are you kidding?"
"No."

"What have you been drinking today?"

"Dr. Pepper, the first choice of grad students."

"Who knows what will happen?"

"*The Shadow*?"

"Mendoza will never buy it."

"He did, yesterday."

"What?"

"I'm a good salesman."

"And Rio?"

"I have to bring him back chocolate cookies made by the college's famous culinary department."

"Some bribe."

"He gets to eat the evidence."

"That leaves me."

"What will it cost me?"

"Three beers on Friday."

"Done."

I had been thinking about the tour for a long time. Almost to a person, my gang buddies never went to the high school's College Advisement Office, even when I suggested it. For whatever reason, they seemed uninterested. I had to literally take them by hand, and that was a struggle. My guys (I was becoming very possessive) were both oblivious to and ignorant of college possibilities. I intended to remedy that.

Fortunately, the husband of our college adviser was a geology professor at the college. He arranged for everything. Still, convincing was needed.

"That's it gentlemen. I need the trip slips by Wednesday."

"Valley College is supplying a bus?"

"Big deal."

"You get to miss three classes."

"Better."

"The college is providing us with a nice lunch."

"Things are looking up."

"You get to see the co-ed's walking around in short dresses."

"We're in."

The trip came off without a falter, though a few Valley College students must have felt like a gang invasion was taking place. I think it was all those bald heads. Fortunately, it was a beautiful spring day with a light wind sufficient to ruffle short skirts on appealing young ladies. One savors whatever favors the gods provide.

My guys visited a number of classes and talked with tough Hispanic students who had fought their way out of the barrio. I can't say the tour changed the world. But I can say that five seniors in the group enrolled in the coming school year. It would be nice if the story ended here. Sadly, it doesn't. Within two weeks, bullets were flying in the barrio and two of my guys were shot. One would never go to college, or anywhere.

That's the way it is in my imperfect world where survival is the key to everything.

Chapter 10

Therapeutic Humor

There are many ways to survive in public education. The Ed books are full of suggestions, minus one: humor. Keep that in mind as you read what follows. It might stand you in good stead sometime when really painful situations arise, and they always do.

"Joker."

Rio was on my case. "I don't believe it." Even you wouldn't do that."
"Don't bet on it."
"Christ, if Mendoza heard about it."
"What?"
"He'd ..."
"He's what?"
"He'd have your head."
"Hell, with this headache, he's welcome to it."
"Jenks doesn't even think you did it."
"Unbelievers. All of you."
"Just incredulous."
"Ask Mr. Jones. He was there. He heard everything."
"He did?"
"And?"
"I did it. So accept it. It was funny."

97

Rio squared a look at me and then started to smile before laughter took over animating both his face and belly. "It was crazy."

"And funny?"

"What was funny? Jenks asked as he came into the office.

"What your fellow Dean did."

"Oh that. It was weird, but funny."

"See," I said. "A consensus."

"What consensus?" Mr. Mendoza inquired as he joined us in my now crowded office.

"Nothing important." Rio said as he covered for me.

"Bull, you guys are talking about what he did yesterday."

"You know about that? I asked.

"Hell, the whole school knows about it."

"Really."

"Funniest thing this semester."

"Really."

"Well, there is one exception."

"Really."

"Nurse Hopkins."

"Hell, the whole thing began with her."

With that, they all sat down, clustering around my desk with amused and imploring looks. Mendoza spoke for them.

"Tell us what happened again."

"No. It's no longer funny."

"Yes it is. Now tell us or I'll be forced to write you up."

"Fink to the Principal?"

"No need. He's already heard the story."

"Then why write me up?"

"What the hell, I thought. What harm would it do? The story would probably make the *LA Times* by tomorrow — *Teacher charged with ...*

"If you insist."

"We do," Rio stated flatly.

"O.K."

The Condom King Story

Yesterday's antics actually began a month ago when Nurse Hopkins entered my office in an administrative huff.

"I need your help."

"What can I do for you?"

"Take over."

"Take over what?"

"The condoms."

"What?"

"I won't give them out anymore. The Board can't make me. The Principal can't make me."

"I get it. They can't make you what?"

"Hand out low bidder condoms to promiscuous young men?

"Low bidder?"

"Cheap. Inexpensive. Bottom-of-the-line. Thin. Easily broken. Are you reading me, Dean. The school district tried to save money by ..."

"No need to go on. I read you loud and clear. Sperm heaven."

"What did you say?"

"Sperm wants egg. Sperm incarcerated in cheap elastic rubber. Sperm breakout. Sperm meet egg. Sperm happy."

"Exactly."

"Really?"

This conversation was getting weirder by the sentence. "Let me get this straight, Nurse Hopkins, you want me to hand out condoms you have no faith in rather than doing it yourself."

"Yes."

"Then I would feel guilty, not you?"

"Yes."

"You want to go to Catholic heaven without your soul troubled by condom sins, right?"

"Yes."

"But then I would have the sin."

"Yes."

"You're too agreeable."

I needed a moment to think about all this. As a Jew, if I distributed the condoms, would I miss out on heaven. I needed to check the *Talmud* on that one. Then again, if I controlled the stock of condoms on campus, perhaps my stock would go up, at least with with the masculine population. Something to be considered… But if the Nurse was right, the school district had bought the low end product would I be complicit in unexpected pregnancies. You can see where this was going. But then again I could tell the guys to "double up." That's real security. On second thought, no way I could do that. But what about that tricky sin stiff Nurse Hopkins kept talking about? Did I really believe in sin? Christ, I needed to see the Rabbi about that one. I fantasized explaining all this to Saint Peter.

"Pete. May I call you Pete? Things were tough. Nurse Hopkins wouldn't give out the you-know-what so the boys could you-know-what with you-know-who. Someone had to help them avoid you-know-what.

Pete didn't respond, not even a quiver of the lips, or a twitch of the eye. This guy was tough. I needed to bargain better.

"Pete, here's the deal. "I accepted her offer. I handed out the item in question. I'm guilty. But look, I can handle almost any punishment except one. If there's a Brent's Deli on your reservation, don't lock me out. It's a Jewish thing. And a gastronomical thing… Have you tried their corned beef? Out of this world."

Back in the real world, I said, "O.K. I'll do it. But you owe me. Next time I'm banged up in a fight, don't give me the cheap *Walmart* green soap."

Two days later I'm meeting with three prim ladies from the local Catholic Church. We were discussing the "you-know-what-problem" with the girls. In the middle of our discussion in walk three lovely senior girls carring in six cases of "plastic protection" in plain wrap boxes.

"These are for you," Lass #1 said in a youngish, earthy voice.

"Nurse Hopkins wants you to take good care of them," Lass #2 said with a coy smile.

"She wants you to make sure they're stored appropriately," Lass #3 shared with a triple wink.

"Where should we put these boxes of condoms?" Lass #2 asked.

"By the file cabinet," I replied calmly, and "Tell Nurse Hopkins I'll put my heart and soul into this."

The girls left. The nice Catholic ladies gave me inquisitive looks to which I said, "Where were we?"

What do you do with five cartons of condoms? I requested an additional four drawer cabinet, which I could lock, and stash my stash away. In no time, the word got around; I was the place to go for free dreams. It was sort of like the movie *Field of Dreams*. "If you build it, they will come." I had them and they came, usually on Friday on the Q.T. Generally, the conversation went like this. "Two please." There was little exposition. Occasionally, a kid would ask for five or more. I considered him a broker for the more shy students. And so it went. Now you know the background.

"Nice, but get to what happened yesterday," encouraged the Principal.

I hadn't noticed his stealth entry into my overburdened office until now. That's what happens when you get too caught up in condoms.

"You, too?"

"Why not? I'm entitled. I want to hear this story right from the horse's mouth."

"If you insist, sir."

"Oh, I do."

The What Happened Story

Yesterday was a tough day. Two fights by nutrition. Six kids caught at I-Hop during period 2. Two purses stolen period 3. An overdosed senior during period 4… He went to the hospital. The kid almost died. And three parent conferences before lunch. To top it off, a food fight in the cafeteria during lunch, which caused me to miss my lunch. Fortunately, I caught a couple of burritos mid air. By period 5, I was about to write a referral slip for myself to *Agnew State Hospital.*

"Tough day," Jenks said.
"You picked a good day for *R & R.*"
"I was sick."
"Sick! I would be sick too, with a 110 golf score"
"I didn't hear that the Principal confided."
"Get back to the story," Rio cried.

I had forgotten about my appointment with Mr. Jones during Period 5, who came waltzing in fit to be tied.

"Is this about Jackie?"
"How did you know?"
"You jotted down something on a referral."
"Oh, yeah."
"Here's the deal. I can't transfer her out of your class. I've talked with her mother and Maria will be suspended from your class for two days. She'll do her suspension with me. I'll need some homework assignments for her."

"Is she repentant?"

"She's getting there."

"Getting there? You know what she did?"

"She'll apologize to you when she returns."

"Is that enough punishment?"

"I err on the side of compassion."

Before Mr. Jones could lend a critical response, the office door popped open and *Billy the Kid*, as I now refer to him, stumbled none too quietly into the room.

"I need three," he yelled with great enthusiasm. Three!"

"Easy kid," I said, "save your energy."

"Three."

"I'm not deaf. And perhaps you should apologize to Mr. Jones for interrupting our fascinating conversation."

"Sorry Mr. Jones."

Good kid. Very animated. Looks like he hit the jackpot. My kind of all-American, red-blooded kid, but let's keep that to ourselves. God bless him. I reached into my desk drawer where I kept my reserve supply. It was easier than going to the file cabinet. That's when it happened.

"What? Jenks asked.

"I saw them."

"Saw what? Rio stammered.

"These."

I held out a handful of mustard, relish, and tomato packets from *McDonalds*. I don't know why I did it. I must have been overworked, anxious, too tension-ridden, and obviously underpaid. I needed a laugh and Mr. Jones wasn't providing any. I needed some humor in my life and my first wife's attorney wasn't around. I needed something off the wall. I guess that's why I did it.

"What?" the Principal asked as if he didn't know.
"I handed three plastic packages to *Billy the Kid*

He accepted them with a confused look on his face.

"New wrapping."
"But…"
"We changed the wrapping so you guys wouldn't feel embarrassed. Neat, right?"
"Are you sure?"
"Sure. Squeeze them. Gently."

He did.

"Lubricant."
"I don't know."
"We're trying to avoid unnecessary pregnancy, AIDS, and other romantic adventures. This packaging should do the trick."

I glanced at Mr. Jones. He was beside himself, a scarlet smile sweeping his face as he looked on never saying a word.

"Here, I'll put them in this *McDonald* bag, which I just happen to have. No one will ever know what's inside."

I proceeded to do this much to the wonderment of the kid and myself. "Enjoy yourself," I said as I handed the bag to Billy. Still a bit unsure, he took the bag and headed toward the door. At that point, and for reasons I never understand, I yelled out, *"Ronald McDonald* loves you."

"Christ," said Jenks.
"No need to bring religion into this," I explained.
"Damn," said the Principal.
"I thought we were agreed, no religion."
"Oh hell, what happened next? Rio asked.

What happened next? I rushed to the door and caught my young Casanova with a near stranglehold. "Come back here, kid." Before he could resist, I grabbed the bag and thrust three low-bid condoms into his shaking hands. "Kid, have a great evening. You really deserve one after what I put you through."

Back in the room, Mr. Jones asked what happened. "We made an exchange, so to speak."

"Forget what I was saying about the referral. Do what you think is best."

"Why the change of heart?"

"After that spectacle, I'm open to anything. Anyway, I needed a good laugh and you provided it."

"Happy to oblige. I must have needed one, too."

"That's the story?" Rio announced.

"Everything, unvarnished."

"One question," said the Principal, why did you call him *Billy the Kid*?"

The Principal had to ask.

"Billy was a terror with a six shooter."

That's the story, more or less. The Principal took mercy on me; I wasn't fired. He didn't need a fight with the teachers union. Secretly, however, I think I grazed his funny bone. I'd like to think he needed a little humor in his life, too. As for Rio and Jenks, they checked my desk periodically for items from *McDonalds*, which, if any were found, they tossed into the nearest wastebasket. As for Nurse Hopkins, she always — with evident glee — used the cheapest, most stinging green soap on me whenever she had a chance. Humor, at least in this story, seemed to have escaped her.

Chapter 11

Survival Persona

"We've all had them."
"I hate it."
"Can't blame you."
"What should I do?"

There it was… What should I do? I was talking with a newly credentialed teacher with only a modicum of student teaching, who was having an increasing difficult time with one of her classes. Indeed, seven weeks into the fall semester, she was ready to quit the teaching profession. She wanted to teach, not be a human boxing bag for immature, discourteous, if not disruptive kids in a freshman English class. Who could fault her? No one goes into teaching to put up with behavior bordering on disrespect. Especially new teachers, who, like a comet they just want to blaze their way across the educational galaxy, enlightening minds and making the world a little better place.

"Two possibilities," I said.
"They are …"
"Progressive discipline responses and/or survival humor."
"Let's be progressive."
"As you wish, Susan. I can call you Susan?"
"Yes."

I explained to Susan that *progressive discipline* was really a proportional response to unacceptable behavior.

Susan blurted out, "I don't understand."

"Look at it this way. You've spent considerable time planning your instructional lessons. Right? Of course, right. You want everything to work. You try to prepare for all contingencies: student interest, different responses, and involvement."

"Naturally."

"Do you do the same thing with discipline? Probably not."

"What are you talking about?"

"Susan, do you have a list of do's and don't in your room?"

"Sure."

"Did you send those lists home?"

"The Principal said we had to."

"Did you discuss these rules with your class?"

"Apparently, not enough."

"Did you discuss them with you?"

Susan paused. She had been ready to pounce on my last question, but then she hesitated. "Exactly, what do you mean?"

"Did you lesson plan your responses to violations of your rules?"

"No, not exactly. Why should I?"

"For the same reason Moses asked Joshua to spy on the enemy. To know how to defeat him."

"Again, I'm confused."

"Try it this way… Why does the football team practice for all contingencies?

"To be prepared?"

"Precisely. The team knows in advance what to do, and to be able to do it if necessary. Think of it this way; if a student is talking on his cell phone in class, you want to have practiced your response. Got it? You need to lesson plan your reactions."

"How can I do that? This is my first year of teaching."

"You do what you can do. Slowly you'll learn planning and proportionality."

"Pro …"

"Never drop an A-bomb on the first violation. If you drop it, what's next? The H-bomb? Pretty soon you'll run out of letters. Your response needs to have some relationship to the darn dastardly deed."

"I'm not sure I get it."

"Let's rule play."

Psychodrama

I told Susan I would be the problem kid in her class and to interact with me. That was an easy rule for me. "Just follow my cues, Susan."

"I won't give you my cell phone."

"This is the third time you've used it in class. I've warned you."

"Personal property. You can't have it."

"Give it to me now."

"No."

Susan was quiet. What's your teacher response?" I asked.

"I don't know what to say."

"Come on; think it through. What's next in your arsenal?"

"If you don't give it to me, I'm sending you to the Dean's Office for disobedience and disrupting my class."

"I'm not going."

"Be careful now. If I have to send for the Dean, things will only get worse. Probably a suspension and a parent conference in school."

"You can't make me go!"

"If the Dean comes here that will only make things worse."

"Who cares? I still not going, you witch."

"I'm not sure if you meant witch or the *b-word*, but either way I'll take it as a gender attack. I'm going to my desk to call the Dean on my cell phone. Isn't technology wonderful?"

At that point, I stopped. "Do you see what's happening? You're escalating in concert with what he saying. You're keeping your cool. You're speaking in a low tone, just loud enough for the other students to hear you. You're being fair. You're giving him chances to back off. Remember, most kids want the classroom under control. They really do. But they also are opposed to the humiliation of a fellow student. You walk a tight line between these fires. That's where the practice comes in, what we might call personal psychodramas you run through in your head."

"I think I'm beginning to understand."

"Good. Each semester we all have the class from hell, or at least a few kids with horns. But if you practice what we've discussed, things will be better. Practice in all your classes. Be firm and fair, and most important, consistent. That's your new persona. Students can accept almost any rule if you do this. Now, let's move on to survival humor. I want to tell you two stories."

"Are they good ones?"

"You decide."

The Story of Terry and the Pirates

I was in my second year of teaching in a junior high school with five classes of forty kids per class. Period 3, those were my sugar-kick kids, all 7th-graders in World History. These kids stopped listening ten minutes before class. If a kid could be tripped in class he was. If a kid could be punched, he was. If a kid could shoot spit wads, salvos went flying. If a book could be dropped, or hair pulled, nasty names shouted, guess what? These kids would do it? Quiet reading time was non-existent. Using class time for homework was like sending an arsonist to put out a fire. Get my drift?

"Yes. What did you do?"

"I got lucky."

"Are you going to tell me, or is it a state secret?"

"I like that. You're being feisty."
"I'm interested."

It happened like this. Out of nowhere, one of the kids asked me what I was doing during World War II? Remember now, this was about 1962 and I was only 23. No way I was in WWII. For reasons I'll never comprehend, I said I was a spy. Suddenly, the class was totally quiet. You could hear that proverbial pin drop. I said it again. "I was a spy." One kid had the good graces to ask the next question. "What kind of spy?" That did it.

"I was a secret spy."
"Really?"
"Would I deceive you?"
"What did you do?"
"I can't talk about government secrets."
"We won't tell anyone."

I looked around. Everyone was looking at me. No disruptions. No stupid stuff. What was going on? I decided to take a chance. "If you promise not to tell anyone ..."
"We promise."
"In blood?"
"Yes!"
"Your blood, not mine."
"Yes!!!"
"O.K., I'll take the last five minutes to tell you one spy story if you get your work done beginning now."

I held my breath. Would these creatures of the deep see through my con game? To my ever-lasting surprise, they hit the books, not each other. As they did so, I was hit with a terrible thought. What would I tell them?

Quiet time flew by. Work was done. Books were closed. Spy time was at hand.

"I was with the OSS, the Office of Strategic Spying. I was aboard a submarine, the *USS Nautilus* off of Tokyo Bay, 1943. It was my job to steal ashore and report ..."

I used up the entire five minutes on my daring mission into the heart of the Japanese empire. The next day the kids were on time and reasonably disciplined when one youngster said, "Can we have another story?" Being brilliant, I said, "Sure, but only after we finish our lesson for today." Bang. Did those kids hits the books as I quickly consider another story.

"After escaping from Japanese imprisonment, I fled to China on a junk, hopped an old Ford tri-engine plan to Shanghai before meeting up with the *Flying Tigers...*"

And so it went. Each day they did their work. Each day I shared another high adventure. My spy persona was now in high gear. It got to the point where I no longer made lesson plans for those kids. I was reading every *Terry and the Pirates* comic book I could find. What was *Captain America* up to? Where was *Plastic Man*? What was happening at the *Daily Planet*? I needed source material. Churchill's History of the *Second World War* was too limiting for my escapades. Eisenhower's dramatic *Crusade in Europe* was like a synopsis compared to my needs. I needed ideas. After all, how many times can a spy leap out of low flying plane on D-Day, capture Russian agents in Moscow, or save a bewildered but beautiful "babe" in Paris?

"You're putting me on," Susan said.
"Would I do that?"
"You might."
"I'm not. I'll swear on a stack of *D.C.* comic books."
"It worked?"
"For me, yes."

"For me?"

"If you're a good storyteller."

"I just might try it."

"Good survival humor, as I call it, can't hurt."

"Any other tip?"

"Watch out for the unexpected."

"Like what?"

"Open House."

As I explained to Susan ... I assumed some of the kids told their parents about my spy stories. At some point, I'm sure suspicions must have been aroused. Even the kids must have suspected that I wasn't a super spy, or any kind of spy. I think there was a tacit agreement with the class, spy stories for good behavior. Then came Open House. The parents took one look at me in all my 23-years of life and realized the obvious. But no one said anything. If their kids were happy and learning something why spoil a good spy story.

"Did you ever do that again?" Susan asked. "Survival humor?"

"Would you like to hear my NASA space stories? I was on the planet Mars where I first met Bing, an escaped robot from the outer ring of the constellation of ..."

Susan declined to enter my intergalactic world and left feeling better, I hoped. Later, when I found her suffering from clinical depression, I would share two more short and sweet stories.

The Heated Room

The two most difficult school periods are 3 and 5. First period your students are still waking up. By sixth period they're rung out. Period 2 they're awake and kicking, same for Period 4. But 3 and 5, these are the NASA periods because the kids are high on sugar, the latest gossip, and music from the dark side. They come into class following nutrition and lunch juiced up. If your 3 and 5 classes are already a task, well you can see where this is going. To deal with this, I had to take extraordinary steps one year. See what you think.

I was teaching in a bungalow, a temporary one built during the last ice age. I noticed I could control the heater for the room: up, warmer, down, cooler. This gave me an idea that worked well with Period 5 in particular. I encouraged my students to have a good lunch and don't be afraid of overeating. At the same time I turned up the thermostat and closed the windows at the beginning of lunch. By Period 5 the bungalow was in sauna land. In theory the kids would come into the hot and humid room on full stomachs, and this would slow down their sugar kick. To complete the deal, I wore a light sweater. Here's why.

There was always one kid who said, "Isn't the room pretty warm?"
This inquisitive, climate change individual would generally add, "Can we open a few windows?"

"Really, you're warm?"
"Yes."
"I'm surprised. I'm wearing a sweater because I'm cold."
"It's 98 degrees outside!"
"Really? (My all purpose response)
"Yes, the room feels like the Sahara."
"Not the Polar Cap?"
"No!"

Of course, I gave in quickly, turned down the heater and opened the windows. If the Almighty was compassionate the worst of the sugar kick was in the past.

The Wastebasket Ploy

This tactic requires a high degree of stage presence. It works this way. You place a full wastebasket behind one of the doors to your room. On the first day of school you meet your students outside of the room. This is really important. Once they've gathered together, you unlock the room and enter. With the kids watching, you kick the staged wastebasket while yelling loudly, "Who put that damn thing there." The kids take notice of your evil side. No discipline problems in theory. Ex-field goal kickers in the NFL swear by this technique. Though I played soccer I'm not a big fan of this business. I'd probably miss the wastebasket and fall on my backside, never a good thing to do the first day of school.

Chapter 12

Off-the-Cuff Humor

"No way."

Sometimes humor just happens, at least that's my best explanation for what happened when Tony, a happy-go-lucky junior was sent to my office for forging a note from home to clarify why he wasn't in school the day before. Actually, the note was pretty good: *"Tony had a temperature of 101 and chest congestion, plus loose bowels."* Of course, Tony neglected to mention surfing off Huntington Beach with like-minded buddies, who wanted to take advantage of especially nice rollers. Our on-the-ball attendance clerk grew suspicious of Tony when she noticed his delightful sunburn. And to my office he was sent.

"Tony, did you cut out of school yesterday?"
"Me?"
"You."
"No."
"Did you hit the surf?"
"Me?"
"Anyone else in here?"
"No."
"Tony, how about this. I stand you on your head and let's see how much sand pours out of your ears and any other orifice."

Tony thought that one over for a moment wondering if I would really do it. Or perhaps he was estimating how much sand was still clinging to remote areas of his sunburned body. Fortunately, fear over came stubbornness.

"I surfed."

"Good waves?"

"The best."

"Next time use suntan lotion big time. You look like a lobster."

"Yeah."

"What about the note?"

"Mom doesn't know."

"Want to bet?"

"She does?"

"Spoke to her after the Attendance Office referred you to me."

"I'm dead."

"No, just sunburned."

"She'll kill me."

"No, she'll buy you *Sea and Ski* for future weekend surfing."

Looking at Tony. I couldn't help but reflect on my own misadventures in high school, where an occasionally cutting school was almost a rite of passage. But what should I do? Tony was doing well in school; he was a first timer with me. Teachers like him. He was on the swim team. Why not? Fresh water in the pool and salt water off shore… All in all, he was a nice guy, who enjoyed surfing.

"Tony, I'm going to cut you some slack."

"Thanks."

"Hear me out before you thank me. I need a letter of explanation and apology to your mom, and the A.O."

"No problem."

"Two hours of community service in school."

"Doing what?"

"Cleaning this office and my colleague's after school this week."

"Cleaning?"

"I'll supply the cleaning materials. You'll supply the muscle. Deal?"

"Deal."

Ah, another successful moment in the life of a Dean, assuming that all went very well. Now, if you're wondering about the *off-hand* humor, don't fret. Just keep reading.

"I think we're done here, Tony. Stay in the waiting room until the bell rings."

"Thanks."

As Tony got up to leave, he noticed what I was doing. Because of edema in my right leg, I wear a pressure stocking, which like pantyhose, tends to slip down my stem. Tony saw me pulling up the brown-colored stocking.

"What's that?"

The truth would have sufficed. "Tony, I have a nylon pressure stocking to assist my blood circulation." But, of course, I didn't say that.

"I have a wooden leg, Tony."

"No way."

"Sadly, yes."

"That's not a wooden leg."

"Are you questioning my integrity? This is a wooden leg."

"It doesn't look like a wooden leg."

"What does a wooden leg look like?"

"You're putting me on."

True, I was putting him on. The funny little man inside me wanted to be funny outside of me.

119

"Tony, I'll prove it to you."

"Prove it."

"Stubborn, aren't you?"

"Prove it."

O.K. I took my right hand and held it near the leg in question. At the same time, I placed my left hand under my solid walnut desk.

"Watch this ... Actually, just really listen."

I hit both my leg and the desk at the same moment. A beautiful walnut wood sound emanated in the room to Tony's utter surprise.

"You do have a wooden leg."

"A believer, at last."

"Wow."

"My sentiments, exactly."

"Wait until I tell the guys."

This I had not counted on. Telling the guys was like telling 3,500 students.

"Tony, I need a favor. Let's keep this between us. If the student body knew I had a wooden leg, the speed characters would never slow down when I yelled, "stop." In a fight, someone would probably trip my timbers. And who knows, some kid might start a fire to singe my wood. The possibilities are endless. What'd say, buddy? Can this be our little secret?"

I waited while Tony considered the situation. If he blabbed, how would I ever explain this to my Principal? Would the faculty ever vote for an imitation one-legged pirate to be Dean? Would I receive threats written on sandpaper? Was I headed for Dean oblivion in some local lumberyard? Or would Tony have mercy?

"Our secret," he said. "You treated me right," he continued. "I'll do right by you. Just take it easy on the office cleaning."

"I'm already lightening your community service."

Tony left the office and I swore to never do off-the-cuff stuff again. Of course, I had made that promise before.

Chapter 13

The Hair Piece Caper

"Boring."

I had to agree with my government students. The blank looks on their faces told all. This educational film had been just that, B – O – R –I – N – G. Even I had almost fallen asleep during the film. It was a sort of electronic water torture, what folks today might call *"water-boarding"* on a screen. This film was guaranteed to put every licensed anesthesiologist out of business. Believe me, dead people would climb out of their graves to avoid this film. Sleeplessness was over in Seattle with this baby.

"Bury that film," a cute blond in the front row said.
"How deep?" I countered.
"Deep."

O.K., some films bomb. No big deal. But what happened next was totally unexpected. The cute blond said, Dr. Livingston, did you get a haircut?"

Students notice everything. A new tie… Lost pounds … Found pounds … Clinical depression … A fight with your spouse … Nothing escapes them, including a haircut.

"Well, not exactly."

Why had I said that? Not exactly; what was the little man inside me cooking up this time? In retrospect I think he was trying to help me. You know, get me out of a tough spot.

"It's a …"
"A what?"

Bending over, I spoke in hushed tones. "It's a hair piece."
"A hair piece," she exclaimed at the top of her lungs. "You wear a hair piece?"
"Not so loud."
"That's not a hair piece," she said.

By now, the entire class was listening, acutely listening, following every word, and peering eagle-eyed at my hair.

"I'm a little embarrassed to talk about this."
"But we've seen you with longer and shorter hair. That can't be a hair piece."
"I have three hair pieces — short, medium, and long. I wear them according to my hair growth calendar."

The class was stunned. In unison, the more sophisticated said, "You have three wigs." As for the savages, "You have three rugs?"

"Hair pieces," I reminded them.
"Prove it," someone said.
"How?"
"Let Cynthia (the cute blond) pull on it. A wig will come off."

What was I to do? The little man had gotten me in trouble again. Maybe I could fake it.

"It's a very expensive hair piece made specially for me to adhere to my head."

"Your bald spot," someone croaked.

"Well, yes, if you must characterize my cranium that way."

"Glue?"

"A new NASA product. Better than glue."

"I can pull it off," Cynthia chimed.

"Give it a try," I stupidly suggested.

Though she was on the small side, Cynthia was a track runner with strong hands. She grabbed two large handfuls of hair and yanked. The hair stayed in place, but not the pain radiating throughout my head.

"See, I told you so," I said. "You can't pull it out."

Boy, was I a dummy. Cynthia regrouped, placed one foot on her chair, and took a deep breath before pulling for her life. My hair fought to go up with her hands, my body levitated from the chair in kind, and the pain hit 1,000 on a scale of 1 to 10, 10 being highest. Still, the hair held. Cynthia released me.

"Isn't NASA great," I said as my nervous system adjusted to the stimulation.

Before Cynthia could answer and try again, the heavenly school bell rang to end the period. As the students left, a common refrain was, "Boring film, but great side show."

As a teacher, or Dean, you take what encouragement you can. Years later, I met Cynthia in a *Ralphs Supermarket*. I couldn't restrain myself. The little guy was still alive and well. "Want another try?" Cynthia's eyes widened and a feral smile appeared. I could almost see saliva whetting her lips. Before she could answer, reality took over. "Only kidding." And we both laughed.

The Blood Test

"It will hurt."

"It won't."

"They could take too much."

"Can't happen."

"I could catch something."

"They take precautions."

I was standing in the quad at lunch with a pint-size, freckle-faced kid and his buddy, a long sliver of a kid who was on the basketball team. Both seniors and 17-years of age, I had asked them if they would participate in the school's yearly blood drive. They had certain reservations.

"I'll die," said Pint-size.

"You won't die."

"My energy level will decline," Sliver stated anxiously.

"Only temporarily. One hour at the most."

A Dean has many jobs, one of which is to push drives: food drives, can drives, conservation drives, clothing drives, beautification drives, and blood drives. All were for good causes. And I pushed all of them hard.

"Come on, guys. There's a real shortage out there. People need blood.

"I do, too," Sliver countered. "Real bad."

"Suppose your best friends were in an accident and needed blood. Wouldn't you help?"

Pint-size remarked, "I send them a get-well card."

"Suppose it was family?"

"An expensive card," Pint-size offered.

These two were pushing me. My competitive juices were flowing. I wasn't going to lose these two red-blooded Americans without a real fight.

"You two never laughed at my jokes in Economics before I became a Dean, right?"

"Dumb jokes," Pint-size quipped. "What did you call a *boycott*?"

"A place where only a guy can sleep," I said.

"See. Dumb."

"What about your definition of *unskilled labor*?" Silver asked.

"What about it?"

"How stupid. A woman having her first baby."

"Well, it couldn't have been a guy."

"See, that's what I mean."

"Then there was the time you told us that the word *picket* had nothing to do with our noses. How lame," Pint-size contributed.

"Actually, I though that one was pretty good."

"It wasn't," they both remarked with painful expressions.

These guys were a hard case. They remembered every joke. They were human tape recorders. All that was missing was laughter on their part. Real sour pusses... I needed to dig deep.

"I'll make you a deal."

"Not another joke," Silver cried.

"A story, sort of."

"What's the deal?" Pint-size asked.

"If you laugh at my story, you contribute blood."

I watched as the two consulted. I could almost hear them ...

"No way he can make us laugh?" Sliver whispered.

"His jokes are awful."

"We can't lose," the long one said.

"Let's up the ante," suggested the small one.

"How?"

"He buys us hamburgers and malts at *Burger King*."

"And French fries."

"Yeah, that, too," petite man said. "He's desperate. He'll go for it."

And I did.

The Bloody Story

I was teaching a U.S. Government class, Period 5. It was just after the noontime blood drive. I waited until all my students were in class, and then, a minute later, entered the class after first poking my eyes.

"Why are you crying?" a concerned student asked.

"I'm upset."

"What about?" inquired another curious student…

"I don't want to talk about it."

"Tell us," a third kid demanded.

"I embarrassed."

"Don't be." they all clamored.

The fish was on the hook. I had the class set up. My little funny guy was ahead of the curve.

"Promise you won't laugh."

"We promise," a chorus of wildly interested students now pledged.

"I hope I haven't misplaced my trust."

"Tell us."

I moved closer to my students, away from the safety and security of my desk area where I kept my pepper spray, handcuffs, and a pump action canister of bug spray. Only kidding. Don't believe a word I just said.

"Look at this," I said as I pulled out a small card from my wallet. I held the card high in the air, weaving it madly as if trying to get the attention of a jet plane flying at 30,000 feet. "Just look at this."

"What is it?" was the collective response. "What's on the card?"
"You don't want to know."
"Yes we do," was the returning chant. "Yes, we do."
"No you don't."
"Yes, we do."
"Fine. But you'll be sorry."
"No we won't."
"Yes, you will."

With a look of anguish, I turned to the nearest co-ed and said, "I don't know what happened."
"What are you talking about?"
"A studied so hard."
"Studied for what?"
"My blood test. And look, I received an A-. I don't know what questions I missed. I feel so stupid. I studied so hard."

I almost impaled the card on her face. "Look, see for yourself. I'm the teacher. I shouldn't miss any questions."
"He's right. He did get an A- the poor kid said. He must have missed something."

For a moment, there was absolute quiet in the class. Not a word was spoken. The class was like the petrified-forest in Arizona. Then the dam burst.

"He's putting us on, dummies. a future FBI agent yelled. You don't study for a blood test."
"We're idiots," a junior *Dick Tracy* added. "He did it to us again."
"I hate it when he does that," a reluctant *Bulldog Drummond* confessed. "Tricked again."

"See. I told you. You didn't want to know."

At that, my students started to chuckle, then bemused by being taken in again, laughed heartily at what had occurred. They summed up their common feelings, claiming they were victims of a child abuse. I conveyed that thought to my little funny guy, but he just laughed it off. He was incorrigible.

As to Pint-size and Sliver, they just looked at me when I finished the story. Nothing could be discerned from their unflappable demeanor. It was as if they had been neutered on national mating day. "God," I thought. "What do these guys want, blood?" *Burger King* was beckoning. I was prepared to use my last *2 for 1* burger coupons. I had lost.

"That really happened?" asked Pint-size.
"In a way, yes."
"And they believed you? Silver challenged.
"It seems so, at first."

Sliver and Pint-size glanced at each other and then slowly a faint smile teased its way across their faces ending in big grins, and a throaty laugh.

"O.K., you win Dr. Livingston," they announced. "That one was kind of funny."
"Kind of?"
"Don't push your luck."

The guys contributed their blood a week later. As they left Red Cross area of the gym having met *Dracula* first hand, I caught up to them.

"Hamburgers after school today. My treat."

Post Script

Twice in my teaching career I received an end-of-the-year present from a class, a book full of my best jokes. As I thumbed through the pages, I began to notice all the pages were blank. Undeterred by this show of youthful gratitude, I accepted the gift graciously. As to the jokester in me, "I heard, "Don't despair, I'm working on new material."

Chapter 14

Serious Stuff

"I didn't do anything."

"You'll have to come with me."

Two simple utterances... A denial. A command. Who would know where they would lead — how the school would be split apart like a ripe pumpkin — how emotions would flare —how accusations would be leveled. How I almost didn't survive the battle of the ADA cards. Had I known, I might not have said, "You'll have to come with me."

It all started so innocently. I guess it always does. I was wandering around the quad at nutrition just doing my supervisory thing when it happened. Out of the corner of my eye, I saw something, nothing more than a vague image, a little fluttering of plastic, a circle of Hispanic girls about twenty yards away. It was all in an instant.

Deans self-train themselves to look for what shouldn't be, what's out of place, what contrasts with the usual. For example, a kid wearing a non-Van Nuys High hat; was he being creative with his apparel or a possibly a serious intruder? Four guys walking steadfast across the campus; what was up? On this day in question some Dean sixth-sense zeroed in on *"what's that all about?"* Something was not right.

I walked over to the group. I tried to act casual. As I did, there was a scurry of activity. Hands moved fast. Purses and backpacks were being opened, then quickly shut. Conspiratorial voices echoed silently within the group I later learned.

"He's coming our way."
"Quick, hide these."
"Act cool."

By the time I got to the group, virginal maidens awaited me. Five lovely young ladies seemingly ready to sing in the church choir. I was greeted like a long, lost friend.

"Hi, Dr. Livingston," the oldest girl said. "What's up?"
"I'm not sure, Claudia. What's up with you girls?"
"Just kicking."

Checking out the girls indicated nothing. Maybe I was overreacting? Maybe my Dean senses were misleading me. Maybe … Then I saw it. On the ground was a piece of plastic wrapping. I bent and picked it up much to the consternation of those around me. It was just a piece of torn plastic wrapping, but printed on it were dreadful words: *LAUSD Admittance Slips.*

LAUSD — Los Angeles Unified School District — four simple words, which would cause all hell to break out.

In Los Angeles, as in other school districts in California, funding is partially a function of *ADA*, or the average daily attendance at a school. To determine the ADA, re-admittance slips are issued when a student returned from an absence. Classroom teachers used these forms to officially record absences. As such, these forms were district documents related to funding. Forging such documents had serious implications. And that's where the rub came in.

"I need all of you to come to the Deans Office now."

"What did we do?" was their communal response to my request.
"Now, ladies."

Grudgingly, they trekked their way to my office. In the presence of
a school secretary and Officer Rio, the girls emptied their purses and
backpacks to reveal an abundant number of ADA forms. Suspensions
were immediately made, which resulted in unhappy parent conferences,
especially with the dads who needed to strut while protecting their
daughters.

"Your daughter was in the possession of stolen legal forms."
"She never used them."
"She didn't have the opportunity."
"Our daughter would never do that."
"Maybe. Or perhaps she was going to give them to other students."
"You can't prove that."
"Correct. Conjecture on my part."

In truth I couldn't do much more than the suspension. Still, I had
to lay down the law.

"If there is another serious incident, participation in the prom and
the graduation ceremony will be endangered."
"There won't be another incident.
"Let's hope so."

All the parent conferences went like that with the exception of
Claudia's. Both dad and mom came in with a boulder size chip on their
shoulders.

Dad led off the conversation … "Why are you persecuting our girl?"
She didn't do anything."
"We'll see. Claudia, where do you T.A. Period 3?"
"The Attendance Office."
"That doesn't mean anything," her father interjected.

"Perhaps. Claudia do you know what the ADA forms are used for?"

"Yes."

"Did you file completed forms away? Is that one of your jobs?"

"Yes."

"That doesn't prove anything," the angry father shouted at me.

"That's to be determined. Claudia, how did you get a package of 500 ADA forms?"

"Someone gave them to her," her mother offered.

"Who, Claudia?"

"She doesn't remember," the mother answered.

"Claudia, you don't remember?"

"Yes."

"Someone who works in the A.O.?"

"I don't know."

"A friend?"

"Just someone."

"Male or female?"

"I'm not sure."

"You're not sure about the gender?"

"Yes."

"A Van Nuys student?"

"Yes."

"Would you recognize the student?"

"Maybe."

"From our book of I.D. pictures?"

"I don't know."

I had to square with the parents. Unless Claudia was more helpful, I could only reach one conclusion: she stole the ADA forms from the A.O. She distributed them to her girlfriends, who would have given them to others. Most probably, forgeries would have followed and the school's funding would have been impacted. Officer Rio would have to be involved.

Even the most devoted and supportive parents have to give up the ghost at some point.

"Tell him, Claudia," her mother encouraged. "Tell him who gave you the forms."
"I can't."
"Claudia." Her father was speaking now. "Tell him."
"I can't"
"Why not?"

With that Claudia burst into tears. "Because I took them."

Case closed. Game over. History moves on. But first, what to do with Claudia? She had never been in trouble. She was getting good grades. She was about to graduate and head on to community college. All and all, a good kid before temptation intervened. Later we would discuss the reasons for her actions, all very personal and not for public consumption. In any event, I had to act.

"I am not going to O.T. Claudia to another school this late in the school year," I told her parents. There will be no Opportunity Transfer. She will be suspended for stealing and lying. She will not be arrested."
"Bless you," her mother cried out."
"I can use the blessing, but I'm not done. I'm recommending that Claudia not attend the school prom or participate in the graduation ceremony. She will graduate, but she will not walk."
"You can't do that," her father said.
"I can and will."
"You're an awful man," Claudia's mother said.

There goes my blessing, I thought.

"You have the right to appeal this decision to the Principal. He will be back in three days from a conference in San Francisco."
"You bet we will," her excited father thundered. "Just watch us."

"I will. Until then, Claudia will be readmitted to all her classes after serving her suspension."

The next three days were right out of *Dante's Inferno*. First came a contingent of Claudia's female teachers. Generally, they maintained that Claudia was a good girl and that she had never been in trouble before, all that I already knew. They added she had already bought her prom dress and ticket, and that relatives were flying in for graduation. Did I really want to ruin all that?

"You're being unfair," her Spanish teacher said.
"Give her a break," the Algebra teacher pleaded.
"What kind of bully are you?" her English teacher asked.

What could I say? Where student forgeries had happened before, these three had been on my case for being too soft. Now I was too hard. To a lady, they were against stealing, but somehow lifting ADA forms were different.

"I'm just doing my job."
"Well, you're doing it wrong?" they echoed as a group.
"And we won't vote for you again," they proclaimed. "And we're going to tell everyone how terrible you are."

The next day Father Gonzalez paid me a visit. He was from the local Catholic Church, Our Lady of Lourdes. Mr. Morales came with him. He was from the Hispanic League. Dr. Hector Pena rounded out this trinity. He was from downtown. You can guess the topic sentence. Father Gonzalez got the ball rolling.

"We would like you to reconsider your decision."
"I have, and it can be appealed to the Principal."
"Perhaps we could avoid that."
"Only if you don't want Claudia's parents to appeal."

Mr. Morales was next. "Some believe you are motivated by a dislike of Hispanics."

"Only students holding stolen ADA forms."

"All the girls involved are Hispanic."

"That's not why they were all suspended."

"You appear to be a prejudiced Anglo."

"Appearances can be deceiving."

"The community doesn't see it that way."

"Their problem."

"And the school's if a civil rights case were filed."

"It's a free country. File away."

I realized I was being testy, but I didn't like the accusations and hardly veiled threats. Into the picture now stepped Dr. Pena. He wanted to make nice.

"I'm sure we can avoid that sort of unhappiness. Don't you think so, Dr. Livingston?"

"I'm not suing anyone."

"Precisely. Perhaps a review might be in order to tweak the punishment ever so slightly."

"I like tweaking. What do you have in mind?"

"Perhaps considerable community service to off-set prom attendance and graduation participation. And, of course, a letter of apology to you."

What to do? Was I being too harsh on Claudia? Was this business worth a knockdown fight with everyone? Would the Principal back me up? I knew Jenks would, and Rio, and Mendoza. But what about my boss; would he stand up to the heat?"

"An apology to the school, not me. She admits to stealing the forms and giving them to her friends knowing forgeries might occur, plus lying to me."

"Perhaps we could tone down the apology a bit."

"Well, she has to apologize for something. She can't just say, I apologize and sign her signature on a blank piece of paper. My god, she has to say something."

"She will."

The Three Wise Men had made their points. "Stick to your guns, Dr. Livingston, and initiate World War III." To satisfy these characters meant jeopardizing the independence, such as it was, of the Dean's Office. I was too stiff necked to do that.

"Gentlemen, I've done my job as well as I could. An appeal process is open to Claudia's family. I encouraged them to take it. And, please, one other thing; stop trying to intimidate me. I'm a member of UTLA in good standing and my union will fight any violation of the contract with respect to my actions as Dean. Do you understand me?"

My words were tough, but my rapid heartbeat conveyed another visage. What had I really gotten myself into?

Three days later, my Principal got me off the hook. He rescinded my actions and gave Claudia 200 hours of community service on campus. It was a good lesson for me. Where serious situations existed and severe penalties were pronounced, politics was always present in the Dean's Office, as it is in the classroom. My friendly jokester passed on this one. There was nothing funny about what happened.

Chapter 15

Seniors Rule

"They're killing each other."

An unexpected call came in from the Girls P.E. Office. A visibly upset and shrieking voice had passed on the unhappy news before slamming down the phone. A hurried return call on my part led to a business signal. What the heck was going on? Was this the real thing or kids working a prank? No way I could take a chance. I quickly reported the situation to my colleagues, most of who were locked up in an awards ceremony in the auditorium. It was Period 4 and the Principal was handing out good citizenship and attendance certificates. I was manning Fort Apache pretty much on my own except for two hired college students who were supervising the halls.

I dashed out of my office and started running toward the P.E. offices, which were at the far end of the campus. It would be a long run for an old guy, a very long way. It would also be a challenge to my campaign promises. "Though a senior, I'm young enough to keep up with these kids." Now that was true as long as the kids were trapped in a telephone booth, not running free on the Great Plains.

Who was I kidding? Flying past the Music Building, I was already gasping air. My heart felt like a Tommy gun and my legs felt like welded lead pillars. Beads of sweat formed on my face and threatening to drench my newly pressed and sparkling Arrow dress shirt. Besides that, it was 97 degrees outside and humid. And I longed for my air-conditioned villa. "Why today?" I yelled. "Of all days."

Ahead of me were our two college aides, loping along at a leisurely pace as if they had no cares in the world. "What the hell is this?" I remarked aloud to myself. Apparently, my urgent request on the "brick" to respond to the P.E. area had not awakened any sense of an emergency on their part. "Unbelievable," I said to the world. "These guys look like they're running in the La Brea tar pits. I need to change this."

But how was I do this? Shame them. Stick it to them. With a flourish, which impressed even me, I blew past my youthful aides, yelling, "Follow me, boys." That accomplished my goal. No way these two husky young specimens were going to let me out run them. The race was on.

Unknown to me Jenks and Rio, after removing themselves from the auditorium, had taken up the chase. From a distance, they saw me grab the lead from the huskies. I never heard Jenks say, "Go old man." Rio was more succinct. "I don't believe it." And unknown to all of us, the Principal, not wanting to be left behind, was also running flat out. He was into the spirit of the thing. No senior citizen was going to beat him to the "killing grounds." In fact no underling was going to out-run him. Title and pay scale have their place.

Dashing around two old temporary bungalows, I spied the P.E. fields only a short distance away now. Glancing back, I saw my two red-faced aides pouring it on, gaining with every step. Close behind them, Rio and Jenks, sirens blaring and lights flashing, were in a sprint. Past them but closing fast was the Principal, 250 pounds of muscle and sinew pounding along the cement walkways. All this should have been filmed. AARP should have been making a documentary.

No one seemed to care about a possible knife or gun infested fight. This was no longer about kids killing each other. This was no longer about panicky phone calls to the Dean's Office. This was personal. This was the *Kentucky Derby* of Deans, aides, and administrators. "And they're off …" This was Indy 500. "Start your engines, gentlemen." This was the L.A. Olympics. "On your mark …" This was a blood sport. Second place didn't count. There was no glory in being runner up.

I held a bare 20-yard lead as I finally approach the P.E. field. Waiting for me were two female teachers. Each held unhappy girl by the neck. With a final kick I arrived, totally out of breath and an excellent candidate for Kaiser Hospital emergency. After taking a huge gulp of air, I said in my most calm manner, "You called, ladies?"

"No problem," a former diving champ said. "We broke up the fight. No one was hurt."
"No problem. How nice" I replied.
"You sure got here fast," the other teacher remarked, herself once a sprinter for UCLA.
"Didn't I?"

At that moment, General Patton (the Principal) and his officers (Rio and Jenks) arrived along with the dog soldiers (the aides). We need to keep things clear here.

I decided to take charge before I passed out. Straightening my backbone and breathing through my ears, I said with an air of authority. "No problem here. It was just a silly girl fight, probably over some boy, who promised ever-lasting love to both of them. Ripped blouses and pulled hair, but no blood." I said all this in one breath. I then calmly walked away with distain. If you're going to flaunt a fiction, you need to do so with an air of conviction. I had the conviction, but now I needed the air.

Closure came as I said, "Jenks, you handle the details."

A quick backward glance almost made me laugh. All the guys had the same disgusted look on their faces. A Social Security recipient had beat them. An" assisted- living" Dean had won. A senior on Medicare had arrived first. I must admit. I relished their looks.

Fortunately, they didn't see what happened next as I rounded a good sized wooden shed, which held PE equipment. There, not visible to them, I bent over in absolute agony, gasping for air like a man emerging from Davy Jones' watery depths. My starched white shirt was now a clinging mess, drenched with my competitive juices. My feet, encased by formerly comfortable, wing-tips felt like heated anvils. God, did they ache.

I slid to the ground with my back up against the shed and closed my eyes. "Lord," I said, "if you take me today, it's O.K. No regrets. But there is just one thing, though. Perhaps you can arrange for a small trophy. Nothing too fancy… I want to remain in good stead with you. Just a small reminder of the race of a lifetime… I'll leave it to you as to what be engraved on it."

It's hard to believe, but I'm sure I heard a baritone type voice say, "I'll take it under advisement."

As I sat there, I realized the potential political points I had just scored, if only the faculty could get wind of it. *"Old man beats Principal to fight."* The fanatics in the teachers union would love that. *"Senior citizen outruns Olympian and police officer."* "The seniors' rule. group would be out of its mind. The near retirement group would go bonkers.

But how should I leak the good news? I couldn't just broadcast it our next faculty meeting. Something more subtle was needed. Perhaps a helicopter drop of 3 X 5 glossy pictures showing my inflated chest hitting the finishing line seconds ahead of my rivals. I shouldn't have concerned myself. P.E students, who had witnessed the spectacle, passed the story on with heroic elaboration. By the time it got around the faculty, I was already anointed the Carl Lewis of Van Nuys High. Naturally, I did little to dissuade those who added to the legend.

But what happened two weeks later was really all that mattered. All the out-footed guys presented me with a great cake on which it was written, "To the Swift." Student reporters were present and a week later there was a great write up in the school paper complete with nice photographs. I realized then how nice it is to have a deity who really took things under advisement.

A month later I won reelection, swamping all other candidates. Perhaps it was my campaign motto: *"He goes the distance."*

Chapter 16

Sweet and Sour Times

A Dean's life is full, sometimes with happiness, at other times with sadness. It was the equivalent of ordering sweet and sour chicken at the local Chinese restaurant. The contrast is always glaring. For example:

Mom on the Warpath

"Why are you always picking on my son?"

I was in my office with an irate Mrs. Wilkinson, a woman of substance and color, who was out for my head.

"Not, always," I said in retort to her accusation.
"You're always calling me when he's out of class."
"When he's cutting class, you mean?"
"Whatever."

Her son, a lanky senior with great track potential, had become a *"drop-in"* student in his last year. Twice a week he would put in an appearance in all his classes, and the rest of the week, he would selectively decide which teachers wouldn't be graced by his presence.

"You never give my son a break. The school has failed him."

"What would you like me to do?"

Mom quieted on that one. Most parents do when you pose the question. "Again, what would you like to me to do, Mrs. Wilkinson?"

"Get him to go to class."
"I've tried. He won't listen to me."
"Make him."
"How?"
"Tell him …"
"Tell him what?"

There we were. Her son wouldn't listen to her. He wouldn't listen to me. He did not fear either on of us. He did not respect us. We had lots of kids like that at Van Nuys High, kids who were defying all overtures. They marched to their own drumbeat; they were on their own.

They were into bad choices and short of running the school like a French penal colony I had little sway in altering their behavior.

"I don't want him to get hurt."
"I don't know what to do." I confessed.
"His father is in jail."
"And your son isn't really in school."
"Can we try again."
"Yes, of course. I'll send for him."

I sent a student monitor for her son knowing full well he probably wasn't in class. And he wasn't.

"He cut third period."
"Where can he be?"
"Let's take a walk."

We needed to get out of the office. It was too confining, too much a reminder of our inability to solve some problems, far more than we dared think. Anyway, if we walked, just maybe we would come across her son. As a Dean you learn in time where the "cutters" congregate. They also learn what you have learned this so new spots are constantly found. It was a *"cat and mouse"* game with no real winners.

We headed out toward the football stadium. Under the stands always made for a good hide-a-way in school. No luck. We headed past some old bungalows and to an area behind the tennis courts. This was a favorite locale for the "pot smokers." Once more no luck… It was like criminality was taking a holiday. A long walk brought us to the far end of the football practice fields. The coast was clear.

"Let's try the baseball dugouts."
"Do you think?"
"Who knows?"

It was worth a try, even if it proved nothing. Apparently, her son wasn't on campus. Nor were a lot of other kids. Perhaps there was a "cutter's convention" in town. What other explanation would suffice?

As we were walking away from the dugouts, I saw a group of students in center field and they weren't playing baseball.

"Some kids over there," I pointed out.

Mom looked intently at the group, distant figures clustered together. It's said that mom's know their kids and that they can pick them out of a crowd. This mom could and did.

"There's my son."

I saw she was right. She yelled, "Come here." No name, just "Come here." If moms know their kids, kids know their moms, or at least the sound of their voice. A face turned in the group.

"Come here now!" she shouted. Nothing.

What happened next needed to be on U-Tube someday. The five boys convened to parlay. In the meantime Mrs. Wilkerson took off after her kid. She was moving pretty good, really eating up the turf. Watching an approaching ticked off mom was not on today's agenda for these guys. They turned and ran for the far chain link fence. Along with his buddies, her son climbed the fence, cleared the top, and then scampered away down side streets once he hit concrete. The speed and agility would have qualified these kids for U.S. Olympic team.

We got to the fence but it was no good. These kids weren't about to be caught by us.

"Why did he do that?" she asked.
"Why does he do a lot of things?"
Neither of us had a good answer. Nor do the sociologists, counselors, and psychologists who pretend otherwise. Oh, they have their theories but when applied to the real world, well sometimes that's another thing. Or at least it was with this mom's kid.

"What should we do?" she asked. It was more a plea than a question.
"The usual, I guess."

The usual; we'd send a truant officer to the home in the evening to talk with the kid. Try to talk some sense into him. Again. Provide counseling. Again. Get the kid to talk to his father in prison. Again. Promise him something. Again. Threaten him. Again.

"I'm sorry I jumped on you. It's not your fault. I know you've tried to help my son."
"I'll keep trying."

The mom left my office. Neither of us had any illusions. Unless something happened her son would simply be another statistic, another dropout Eventually, he would be just another nameless kid on the mean streets of Los Angeles. The whole thing left a sour taste in our mouths.

Disrobing

"Just take off your pants."

What could I say? The Home Education Teacher was insistent. She wouldn't help me if I kept my *Dockers* on.

"Are you sure?"
"I've done this before. Now off with them."
"But ..."
"Don't get excited. I've seen the male form before."
"But not mine!"
"Shy, are we?"

What could I say? It's not easy for a grown man to disrobe in front of a female colleague. But what could I do? She had an arsenal of sharp scissors and an abundance of potentially pointed pins. I wasn't about to tangle with this lady.

How did this embarrassing business begin? Very simply, I had broken up a fight on the quad. In the process I split the backside of my Dockers. It was a big time rip leaving me with unwanted air-cooling and the unwanted attention of some. And, of course, this had to be the day I wasn't wearing a sport coat. I caught up with the Home Economics teacher as she was about to leave for lunch. An emergency I moaned and explained all. Being the lovely woman she was, she took pity on me, which led to her command, "Take toff your pants."

It took her only a few minutes for her skilled hands and a handy sewing machine to patch things together. But those were a long few minutes. Just as she was completing the job, one of her female colleagues came into the room looking for her. One look at me, and she exclaimed with a big, knowing smile, "Split your pants, I see."

"Done," said the Home Economics teacher. "Try them on."

"Now?" I asked.

"You could wait until Saturday," her friend said with obvious delight in my plight.

"In front of …"

"Oh," they each said in teasing voices. "Would you like us to gaze away?"

"Perhaps there's something on the ceiling to capture your rapt attention."

Thankfully, they turned a bit and looked at the room clock. As they did, I leaped into my pants and yanked the zipper. It stuck halfway. I had pulled too hard. The ladies turned and found me fumbling with the hateful metal teeth.

"Having trouble?" one asked in obvious ecstasy at my pitiful plight. "Want some help?"

"Home Economics teachers are trained for anything," the other offered with a glee in her eyes.

"Ladies, I think I'll manage this on my own." With that I pulled with a wing and a prayer and God answered. The zipper obeyed a higher authority and closed nicely.

"Darn" was their mutual response. As I was leaving the room, I thanked Mrs. Johnson for her sewing skills, which saved my pantaloons. To which she said, "Not a problem and by the way, nice legs."

The next day I sent her a bouquet of spring flowers with a sentiment" *"I am indebted, legs and all."*

How sweet life is at times.

Chapter 17

Troubles in Paradise

"See me."

Just two words ... Just two small words on a memo note ... Translation not needed. No explanation provided. The Principal simply wanted to see me. No time was listed. No day was enumerated. Just come to my office. But it meant now, as soon as you can.

As a teacher I had received more than a fair share of these "black spot" notes more akin to *Long John Silver* than educators. Always, they left me with anxiety. I dreaded receiving them. What have I done now? I must have done something. And knowing myself, I probably did some offensive deed. My career was pockmarked with such transgressions. Indeed, it appeared to me that every Principal I ever worked for maintained a singular chair in his office just for me.

It wasn't that I got into trouble on purpose. Trouble just seemed to search me out no matter my yearly resolution to walk "the straight and narrow." Paranoia aside, I was the victim of unruly circumstances, which conspired to envelop me in a world of miscues and misunderstandings. Premeditation was not my bag. I didn't have to plan carefully in order to get into a fix. Much as a magnet does, I merely attracted "sin."

When I became a Dean, I swore I would never send a "see me" note to anyone. That, I might add, was one resolution I did keep. I didn't want others to experience the same fate. Empathy was the operative word here. As an example...

Trouble with Desmond

"But this isn't an English class."

My psychology class was upset. My students didn't want to read and analyze a book related to general psychology. Somehow they believed that writing was confined to English classes. Elective courses were supposed to be fun, where reading and writing were abolished to some locale in Siberia. But I had taken a different stance.

"Do we have a choice in what we read?"

Of course, my students had a choice. A list of 50 titles was given to them, and, if that proved too limiting, a non-listed book was O.K. once I blessed it. Somewhere in the vast universe of literature floating around in our world, whether in our own school library, or from a local college, there had to be something in print for even the most selective of students.

"Why do we have to analyze it?"

Yes, they just wanted to read the book, if indeed they had to do this assignment in the first place. They wanted nothing to do with analysis. What were the themes of your book as they related to psychology as a subject, and how you might apply these notions to your own personal life? Pretty straight forward, I thought. Footnotes note needed... First person fine... Double space typing requested. No more than five pages. Three weeks to complete assignment. Important mid-term grade... You get the picture.

"I found a good book."

Over the next few days my literary resisters located, as I knew they would, just the right book.

"I think I'm going to like this."

Once into their choice, they began to enjoy what they were reading, and, hopefully, what they were learning.

Everything seemed to be going right for once. No traumas had come my way this school year. But it couldn't last. Eventually, a "see me" note would search me out and I would head for my accustomed chair. It did.

Confrontation

"Did you give your class a writing assignment?"

Sitting in the Principal's Office, I considered this dumb question. How could you teach a psychology class without giving at least one writing assignment in twenty weeks? Anyway, when a principal asks a question, he usually already knows the answer. We've been through that one before.
"Yes, sir."
"Was it sort of like a book report?"
"Sort of, yes."
"The students were to apply what they learned to their private lives?"
"To their personal lives."
"No need to cut split hairs."
"As you say …"
"You gave your students a list of books?"
"Yes. May I inquire as to why I am being interrogated?"

Sometimes it's best to be a little aggressive with your boss. "Interrogated" was an aggressive word.

"A parent has filed a complaint."

"Because?"

"His daughter read a book."

"Sounds like he's complaining about every teacher in school."

"Not just any book."

"Are you going to keep me in suspense, Sir?" Another aggressive word…

"From your book list."

"There were fifty books on the list."

"Desmond Morris?"

"An author."

"*The Naked Ape?*"

"The title of his book."

What could a parent be complaining about? Morris' book was a *Book-of-the-Month* selection. It was in our school library, approved by the district's review committee. In scientific, if not psychological and anthropological circles, it was hailed as a break through reading for the general population. It was on the best seller list for months. It described in elegant prose and numerous pictures the place of human beings in the world in contrast to other creatures, especially other primates. What could possible be amiss?

"The parent didn't like chapter 2"

"Chapter 2?"

"Sex"

"What?"

"Reproduction."

"You mean mating?"

"Exactly."

I was confused. Morris had described in non-technical jargon, the mating process of human beings. What could be wrong?

"He didn't want his daughter reading such trash."
"Did he actually read the chapter?"
"No. He refused once he looked at all the pictures."
"Christ. What does he want?"
"He wants me to fire you for forcing his daughter to read porn."
"I'm relieved. I thought he wanted something serious."

Humor is always helpful when the world is collapsing around you. Perhaps not on the tilting deck of the *Titanic*, or in *Hiroshima* after the atom bomb, but certainly in the Principal's Office. It helps to relieve the pressure. Unfortunately, the Principal wasn't in a jovial mood.

"He'll take it to the Board if I don't fire you."
"And that's for openers?"
"He wants your teacher credential voided."

Now this was getting serious. This parent was after my wallet.

"He'll also go after me because I'm your boss."
"Nice guy. What's his name?"
"Brock."

Be honest. Admit it. There's someone in your life you hate, a person you are obsessed with who has stormed into your dreams and preoccupied your waking hours in a negative way. Though a kind and compassionate soul, you fantasize about this person. That is, eliminating him. I certainly did about Mr. Brock.

At that moment I really wanted to be an Italian. I wanted a connection to the mob. I wanted to call Uncle Vince. I fantasized.

"Vince?"
"My teacher guy. What's up?"

I explained.

"You want me to pay him a visit?"
"Oh, yes."
"A little persuasion, perhaps."
"Oh, please."
"A knee, perhaps."
"Only if necessary."
"Done. Be a good boy."

But I didn't have an Italian connection. I was a Jewish kid. How could I convince Jerusalem that Mr. Brock was a Palestinian terrorist? If I could, he might enjoy a long swim in the Mediterranean.

I considered going to his place of work, an insurance company and, acting very crazy, accuse him of anti-Semitism. Anthrax and a letter bomb also found their ways into my fantasies. I even considered hiring BVN for put a "hit" on him. And, you know, they might have taken the contract. I thought about contacting Desmond Morris himself and making this a cause celebre. I even considered getting the most available senior girl to get Brock into a compromising situation. You can see where this is going.

"What are you going to do?" I asked my principal. "Is this the end of our beautiful relationship?"
"I'm consulting with downtown."
"And I'll consult with the teachers' union."

So we did. Over three unearthly months, a deal was worked out. I didn't like the deal, but I did like my job. I hated to compromise on principle, but I had a family to feed and a mortgage to pay. It seems we all have a price. In the end I just wanted the problem to go away.

I had to write Mr. Brock a letter of apology and promise not to use Morris' book again. The book was pulled from the school library and placed in the backroom, where with a parent permission slip it could be used only under the librarian's supervision. A note was placed in my file. It focused on my need for ethical behavior.

You can see, I believe, how a "see me" note is nothing to be scoffed at with the Brocks of the world running around. Unfortunately, that wasn't the end of the story. Round 2 was coming up two years later.

Trouble with Paint

"Turn on the projector," the Principal said in a heated voice. "Let's get this over with."

I was sitting in a crowded Audio-Visual room with my boss, the A-V coordinator, and a downtown representative. I was in trouble again and once more in a psychology class. And again, I had received a "see me" note. How could this happen? In my case, easy… It all started so innocently.

"I have a great film for the last week of the semester," my beautiful student teacher informed me. "Want to review it?

"Tell me about it."

"It concerns communication and how we filter information in order to maintain our focus on a subject of interest."

"Jesus," I said, "the kids will be asleep in one minute."

"Not necessarily," she said.

I should have picked up on that, but I didn't. "Where did you get the film?"

"*CSUN* – California State University Northridge. From the film library, Psychology Department."

"Impressive."

"My M.S. committee chair suggested it."

"It's nice to know people."

"It won numerous awards from the *National Film Association*."

"I can't see a problem. Go ahead. Show it. No need for me to review it."

Dumber words were never spoken. I should have reviewed it, but I trusted my student teacher, now at the end of the semester with mainly seniors taking her Psychology class. But I didn't. I mean there were only two days left in the semester. What could possibly go wrong?

She showed the film the next day. As I graded papers in the back of the room, I watched the film. It was entitled *Paint*.

The film began with a pedantic voice describing the brushes and other materials used by an artist as he goes about preparing himself for a portrait rendering. Within 60-seconds I was falling asleep, along with thirty students. This boring, passionless voice could knock a raving hyena into slumber land. This "voice" made the stillness of a desert night sound like a circus. Had the Pentagon licensed this voice, the enemy would have fallen asleep mid-charge. Strong-willed kids were rocking on propped up elbows. A glazed look seeped into the room and drenched everyone. I was not, as I pointed out, immune.

Back to the film. A door opened to the artist's studio and an attractive, conservatively dressed female entered. Obviously, she was the model. Then slowly, against the backdrop of the monotonous monotone, she began to undress — coat, shoes, blouse. Blouse! Hey, what was going on here? Around the room there was a flustering of heads, a stirring of bodies, a cognitive rebirth as eyeballs focused on the screen. The model was taking off her blouse. Wait a moment… School films didn't show such fare.

Next came the skirt and stockings. What in the world was going on, or in this case, coming off?

The room was deathly quiet except for heavy breathing, which had overtaken these kids. All were fully alert. The narrative voice continued as it described how the artist approached his subject, position her (as in this case) just right for the best lighting and perspective. Who cared? All attention was on the model now dressed only in her birthday suit. How far would this go?

I should have stopped the film at this point. You know, click and the projector dims and dies. If unwilling to be seen as a spoilsport, I should have faked tripping over the extension cord and purposely pulled the plug; it would have been celluloid curtains for *Paint*. If a false fire alarm, which always happened when you least expected it, had gone off, I could have pried the students from their seats with a crow bar and gotten them to safety. Had the P.A. system interrupted with news that WWIII had started, I would have been O.K. No time for frivolous films. Everyone man your battle station. I wasn't that lucky.

The movie ran on. The artist then began paining the nude form in vivid splashes of psychedelic colors. Close ups of the brush at work showed every detail. Heavy breathing in the classroom had given way to shortness of breath and inarticulate muted sounds as students watched in stunned silence. The model was the canvas.

A terrible thought now entered my consciousness. What would happen if the Principal showed up? The Mayor? The Governor? A palpable fear now encroached upon my mind. I would I explain all this? I hadn't previewed the film. I knew then I was chopped liver.

The artist continued to paint, stroke after stroke, while the narrator talked on about the need for just the right brush. Finally, the artist finished his work. The model then moved toward a bed, which we saw for the first time. The cover spread was an exact duplicate of the psychedelic colors on the her. She pulled back the cover and got into the bed. Understandably, but unfortunately, the artist followed her. Then they both disappeared under the covers. Once covered, there was a brief wiggling movement of bodies beneath and the film came to a merciful ending.

The lights came on. Sweaty students gazed at each other. I prayed my student teacher wouldn't, but she did anyway. "How did you like the film?" she asked. That was like asking if elephants cared for peanuts. Do Jews like bagels, or corned beef? Does the NRA like the Second Amendment?

She followed up with, I should add, a great question. "What was the purpose of this film? What was the film getting at? To the first question, there was unanimity of thought. "We liked it." To the second question, there was considerable debate and robust discussion focusing on attention spans and the influence of stimuli on our concentration.

Soon after I received the "black spot."

That's how I ended up in the crypt-like A-V room with my friendly film critics.

"Run it," the Principal said.

The film peered out of the camera lens and flickered on a small make shift screen. You already know what they saw.

"I don't believe this," the downtown voyeur announced as he gazed intently as the undressing model.
"What were you thinking?" my Principal asked in a hushed voice punctuated by labored breathing.

And the A-V coordinator didn't help ... "I can get a better image, greater clarity," he said as he adjusted the projector. "Thanks," I thought. "You're a real friend."

In the middle of our viewing, the door flew open. One of the A-V students was returning from showing a film. He checked us out — and the film — as the Principal frantically slammed the door shut. "Hey," he said in a most animated voice, "that's the great film we saw in Psychology today. Thanks for showing it Dr. Livingston."

I was dead. My red pencils would be taken away from me. My roll book would be confiscated. Access to the cheap cafeteria food was over. Teacher discounts at the mall would be voided. I would never see a retirement check. My life in civil servitude was over.

"How did all this happen?" the downtown guy asked.

I explained, leaving nothing out, and taking full responsibility for the film, hopefully to take the onus off my student teacher who needed her teaching credential. I would be the fall guy. What little honor I had permitted nothing else.

"I'll get back to you in a few days," my boss said in a strident tone.

Two days later, I got another note. I wondered how thick was the Principal's note pad? I sprinted at a turtle's pace to the Main Office.

"Sit down." I did. "We got problems." "We," I thought. "Remember Brock?" I did. "His secretary had a student in your class. She told her mother about the film. Guess who she told?" No need. I knew. She told her boss, this guy Brock. "He's on the warpath and with good reason." At that, my scalp felt itchy. "He wants our job. And mine." Thankfully, my student teacher hadn't been mentioned.

Silence reigned for a moment before I asked, "What are we going to do?"
"You're going to take a hit."
"Another letter of apology?"
"Yes."
"Another warning in my file?'
"Yes. Be careful. A third file warning tied to morality could mean your credential."

"Any other good news?"

"CSUN will not longer let its students, our student teachers, use their film library."

"Christ."

"The only films which can be used must be approved by our district film people. No exceptions."

"Damn."

That was it. To avoid a third file reprimand, I've been scrupulously clean after this incident I previewed every film, book, or handout. Hell, I reviewed the reviews. The system won.

As for Mr. Brock, I never actually met the man. I only felt his presence. He was a shadow hovering over my professional life.

In time I came to understand that, as a Dean, dodging bullets on the mean streets, breaking up drug sales, or stepping into the middle of a fight was much safer then being a classroom teacher. And one other thing; as a teacher always preview everything before you use it in the classroom. Remember, it's always CYA time, survival in three letters.

Chapter 18

Off The Wall Stuff

"God, I remember when you locked us in the head."

Whether they desire it or not, a teacher or Dean becomes an embedded part of the collective memory of students. Sometimes, it was what you said. Sometimes, it was what you didn't say. Possibly it was a shrug or look, which entered the universe of a kid's life and remained there. It's a sort of lingering memory, a special reflection of institutional notoriety. And I had my fair share of it.

Smoker Heaven Disrupted

"We can't breathe."

It was true. I had locked the door to the boy's head and the smoke-filled room made it hard to breath. Given the natural, if not indigenous smells of this tiled land, maybe that was a good thing.

"This is crazy," a burly high school senior stammered.
"You were warned, Steve."
"We never thought you would do it?"
"Never underestimate a pissed off dean."

As I spoke, I threaded the final loop of film into a 16mm projector. O.K. guys, as advertised, you're going to see a 3-minute film on the dangers of smoking brought to you by the *American Cancer Society* and me.

"It smells in here."
"Urine, crap, and smoke, I agree."
"You can't do this!"
"Watch me."

I clicked the on lever and a hazy black and white film appeared on the wall of a stall. The *Egyptian Theater in Hollywood* this was not. No comfortable chairs. Just eight or nine guys standing in the haze, all really considering me a "dick."

In short order the film was over. "O.K., you either got the message or you didn't. You'll either continue smoking or you won't. If you give up the smoking habit, great I applaud you. If you don't, that's your business unless you smoke on campus, or more to the point, in this head. Then it's my business. Now, out of here."

As my addicts to Madison Avenue's unrelenting sales pitches left, I gave each one a pamphlet about the harmful effects of smoking, which they grudging took. I had no illusions. Peer pressure and juvenile defiance were powerful forces in a teenager's life. And Hollywood didn't help with all its leading men dangling tobacco from their lips. The many sporting events sponsored by the *Marlboro Man* were tough competition. But you try. What else can you do?

"That was a crazy deal," I said.

"Off the wall," the burly well-dressed young man said. "What was it? About five years ago?"

"Something like that, I guess."

"I told my mom about it. She laughed. One or two cigarettes a day were her limit. My dad was a two-pack man then. He was really upset with you. My mom talked him out of paying you a visit in school."

A few years had passed, but I was beginning to recognize the face.

"Steve, isn't it?"
"You remembered."
"Yeah. It's good to see you. What are you doing these days?"

We were standing in the DMV parking lot in Canoga Park. I had gone there to renew by license. I strained on the eye test and killed the written examination. I was good to go if I wore my distance glasses. Steve saw me about to unlock my car. He told me he worked for the DMV and that he was doing well.

"Glad to hear you're doing well. Steve, I can't resist the impulse. The guy who took my picture... I asked to take me smiling. He didn't. He used the camera like a '45.' Bang! I look like I've had one too many drinks. I've seen better wanted-pictures in Post Offices. Can you transfer him to Elba Island or Okinawa?"
"We don't have an office there," he said with a big smile. Sorry."
"No problem. Anyway, something else is on my mind. "Did you ever quit smoking?"
"Not at first. But then my dad got real sick."
"I'm sorry."
"Cancer got him."
"It gets a lot of people."
"That's when I quit."
"I'm glad."

It was time to switch subjects.

"Girl friend, Steve? Married?"
"Engaged."

"Kind of like being in escrow."

We both laughed. "I need to be off. Good to see you again, Steve."
"Same. Only thing…"
"Yes?"
"Thanks for trying."

I smiled and drove away. We were both a long way from the "head."
But the memories remained. Maybe what we say and do is important.

Another Chance

"Not you again!"

I was on the phone with Mrs. Friedman, a really terrific lady, who
was the principal of a small storefront continuation school not far from
Van Nuys High.

"Yes, I'm afraid it's me, Mrs. Friedman."
"And, I suppose, you have another hardship case for me?"
"All my cases are hardship situations."

Mrs. Friedman's school, which housed a meager 80 students, was
located in an office building near Victory and Van Nuys Blvd. The entire
third floor had been renovated to run an essentially individualized study
program for high school students who were at extreme risk. Leasing
a floor, along with improvements, was cheaper than building a new
school, or expanding an existing site.

"What is it this time?" Pregnant senior? Battered kid? Runaway
junior?"
"No."
"No?"

She sounded fierce, but she wasn't. She came across as an ogre, but she wasn't. Indeed, she had a heart of gold. This was just a little game we played, sort of a way to let off steam. Almost always, if there were anyway possible, she would accept a student I recommended to her.

"She's a senior with one semester left and she needs45 credits to graduate."
"Forty five credits!"
"I have a plan."
"You always do."

In high school, each completed class earns five credits. Usually a student takes 6 classes and earns 30 credits each semester. My referral needed an additional 3 classes.

"She can't stay at Van Nuys High."
"Because?"
"She's from out of state. Idaho. Her father belongs to a Nazi-type group and her mother is an addict. She's living with a grandmother in Panorama City. She had decent grades in Idaho given the situation. But…"
"But?"
"She's a gay white girl coming from a race-baiting family to a mainly Hispanic school. We're concerned for her safety."
"We can't give her 45-credits."
"Thirty-five is fine. I'll also enroll her in Adult School for two classes."
"You do have a plan. Can she do it?"
"She's smart."

I liked this girl the first time I met her and the grandmother. She just needed a chance. Most of us just need a chance. I was in a position to make it happen. The situation appealed to my God-temperament.

"If she graduates, she has a chance. Right now, she wants to do that. I need to make that possible."

"That's why I love you. You're a sucker for a kid coming from a white supremacist home."

"I plead guilty."

"Send her over to me as soon as possible."

I did. I arranged for the transfer and got her registered in Adult School. That was the last time I saw her. Then one Christmas season a few years later, I received a nice card from her. She was living in Florida and working in a bookstore. She was only a couple of classes away from her A.A. degree. She had inked her signature and written a short sentiment — "Thanks." Her card made me feel good. It reminded me that we might live forever as long as people remember us.

The Show Must Go On

"You must be kidding."

I was in the faculty cafeteria with the swim coach, Mr. Knight. He was a former colleague in the Social Studies Department.

"You'll enjoy it," he said.

"No, you'll enjoy it. You've got the body for it — more youthful, athletic, muscled."

"Well, yes, that's all true, but you're in decent shape."

"To what," I stammered. "Assisted living folks?"

"I understand. That is a tough comparison. Perhaps the terminally ill?"

"Some friend."

Mr. Knight was trying to talk me into participating in the upcoming faculty talent show to raise funds for the various teams. The goal was beyond question. Participation wasn't a problem. It was the kind of participation that was the problem.

"A muscle stand-off in *Speed-O's* in front of 1200 students. You expect me to do that?"

"You're the most likely person. You're a great Dean. The kids love you. They'll rush to buy tickets once they know you're in this act."

"Flattery. I bet you're telling this to everyone."
"Right, but in your case I mean it."

Knight was really playing me. I tried to escape from his web.

"Get Jenks. He's younger."
"No. We need a senior vs. youth."
"And I'm the senior?"
"Exactly.
"Get Webster. He's so old he could pass for Daniel Webster."
"The kids don't like his sour breath. Besides, he picks his nose. Kids won't pay hard cash for him. But you, on the other hand ...
"Stop. Tell me again what's involved."

He did. As he described it, it didn't sound too bad. But I knew Knight. He could sell sand to an Arab.

Finally, I gave in with a shudder, I must admit. "Fine. I'll do it."

Finally, the big day came. A matinee performance was held in the school auditorium after lunch for two periods. Many of the faculty participated, as did a host of young people. Every seat was sold. There was talk of scalping in the quad. A rumor, circulated first by Knight, traveled quickly throughout the student body. The old Dean would be in *Speedos*. Sales were brisk as the news spread.

We were the last act. The principal was counting on us to bring down the house. As long as it wasn't my scanty *SO's*, I was O.K. with that. It was time for our act. The M.C. took his time building us up.

"And now, sparing no cost, we have our final act, a muscle posing contest between Mr. Knight, a former Olympian swimmer and our present swim coach competing against a senior citizen, non-other than our favorite Dean, good Dr. Livingston."

The crowd chanted. "Speed-O, Speed-O. The stage curtain pulled back to reveal us in tight-fitting robes standard near a huge bar bell. The crowd exploded with wolf whistles and other unusual sounds.

We turned and faced each other. This was the moment of truth. We partially opened our robes. The noise was louder than before, incessant in nature, and really quite something to hear. I'm sure the kids, and I might add, the parents and secretarial staff, moved the needle over at Cal Tech.

We discarded our robes and stood nearly stark naked in a blaze of stage lights. My god, what had I gotten myself into? We squared our shoulders and looked at each other with piercing looks. As planned, Knight went into a rehearsed pose, which I then attempted to duplicate. The crowd responded with a wave of thunderous appreciation. Over the next few minutes, we taunted each other with various muscle configuration poses. Actually, it was kind of fun.

The M.C. cut in again. "And now, our contestants will attempt to lift this 250 lb bar bell. I went first and faked being unable to lift the weight. Faked? Are you kidding? I would have blown my *Speed-O's* if I were really trying. No way I could lift that iron. Knight's turn was next, and though the bar moved upward a little, that was it. We stood together dejected.

Then came the big surprise for the audience. Dressed in a tight outfit and in high heels, our weight-lifting queen, Miss Jones, from the Science Department, came on stage to give it a try. Gripping the bar, she glanced over at us and grinned before one great lift. Off the stage came the weight chest high before she replaced it on the floor. After a "I told you so look," and a big wink, she left the stage to a roaring applause.

Years later, when I was shopping in the Van Nuys area, it wasn't uncommon for a former VNHS female student to come up to me, saying, "I still remember Speed O contest. You guys were great. And by the way, "Nice buns.""

It seems that notoriety comes in many forms.

Chapter 19

Drugs

"The meat wagon is here."
"Christ, Mike would it kill you to say ambulance?"
"Sorry, Doc. I've been watching too many 1930's detective movies."
"You're forgiven."

Mike preferred Doc to Dr. Livingston, and I did too as long as my paycheck wasn't involved. There I preferred to be more formal.

"The girl still in the Nurse's Office?"
"Yeah, she overdosed alright."

Mike was a paid extra hand, a USC junior hired by the school district to supplement our meager Dean's Office staff. Except for an occasional lapse into the 30's he was a good guy. I think he's a film major. He knows I went to UCLA. Now and then he whistles *"Fight On."* I try not to respond.

"Doc, the paramedics are working on her now. They're trying to avoid cardiac arrest. They've been massaging her chest, trying to keep her respiratory system from shutting down. She's wearing a plastic ventilator."
"What a way to start Monday, Mike."

"It's good thing her science teacher heard her slurred speech and saw her lack of coordinator."

"Right."

Another one… That's all I could say. Another overdose. Another potential high school death… And all I could do is sit back and watch it happen all over again, as regular as London's Big Ben. Another reminder that weekends can be deadly.

"Double check. Let me know when they're ready to leave?"
"Okay. You've called home?"
"Yes."

The worst part of the Dean's job, calling home when a life is at stake. You never get used to it.

"Mrs. Watson?"
"Yes."
"Dr. Livingston, the Dean over at Van Nuys High."
"Has something happened to my daughter?"

Parents have a built in alarm system. The school calls; the system activates. Fear is always the common denominator.

"Caroline overdosed. The medics are with her now. They're stabilizing her. She'll be taken to North Hills Hospital momentarily. I'll go with her in the ambulance. Meet me there in Emergency."

I always try to get that part over quickly. Experience has provided me with a template:

. What happened? Overdose.
. Help? Medics
. Condition? Stabilizing
. Hospital? North Hills

. Assistance? Dean
. Where? Emergency

Not a perfect system, just the best one I had. My phone rang.

"They're ready now, Doc."
"I'm not, but I'll be there."

No matter how you cut it, the ride to the hospital is hellish. Caroline, pale and with labored breathing, was covered in white sheets and a dusty-gray colored blanket. The ventilator still covered her mouth and nose. The medics monitored her vitals as the ambulance maneuvered through crowded streets, siren blaring to warn vehicles and pedestrians — a life was hanging in the balance. In only ten minutes we were at the hospital. Though a bit of a weak-kneed agnostic, I said a little, silent prayer for this kid. Elsewhere I knew what was happening.

"Yes, the school called. She overdosed."
"Bad?"
"Yes."
"I'm leaving work."
"I meet you at the hospital."

And at the hospital a fifteen minutes later.

"Mrs. Watson, let's sit down. Caroline is with the doctors."
"What did she take?"
"I don't know."

Parents always seem to ask that question. I guess I would too. The possibilities were endless: pills (take your choice), alcohol, heroin, prescription drugs, or the latest custom job... And in the end did it matter?

"Where did she get them?"

The "them" was never spelled out, but the question was asked anyway. I guess it had to be. Parents want answers.

"Later, Caroline will tell us."

If the gods of traffic were compassionate Caroline's father would soon arrive. He did. And then the same questions would be asked and the same unsatisfying answers would be given. And again, if the gods were forgiving, the doctor would meet us with the good news.

"Caroline will be okay."

But it wasn't always that way.

"I'm sorry. We couldn't save your son."

Later

"How are you doing, Doc?"
"Pissed and tired, if you must know, Mike. These damned drugs are ruining our kids. They mess with their minds. They kill them. They get them into trouble with the police, and I can do crap about it."

I was venting. Mike knew that. No matter what the school did, the plight continued. Our best efforts had slowed, not stopped the problem. That guy Sisyphus had nothing on us.

"We do our best, Doc."

That Afternoon - Late

I arrived home. One look at me, and my wife knew pretty much what was up. She always knew. A few minutes later I rounded up my "I had a tough day" buddies and placed them on the kitchen table.

There were my prescription painkillers for my back, little white tablets, teasing me. Some friendly tranquilizers to ward off depression silently clamored for my attention. Of course, my old friend, Mr. Jim Beam was there I could almost hear him saying, "One shot won't kill you." I stared at my erstwhile buddies. They stared back, professing innocence, as if to say, "We're here, but we're not responsible for the abuse. So let us off the hook."

My wife watched this ritual. She had seen it before.

"Well?"

Brushing aside the sirens on the table, I got up and walked over to my wife.

"I'd need a kiss and a hug."
"And a tissue."

The tissue was always for that one silent tear I couldn't hold back when even humor deserted me.

Chapter 20

Our Achilles' Heel

"Have you seen my grades?"

"Actually, no."

"A deluge of 'F's!'"

"And you still graduated from Stanford? Unbelievable."

"What are you talking about, Dr. Livingston?"

"My exact question. What are you taking about, Ms. Kilpatrick?"

That's how it all started. Ms. K, deeply depressed by the number of failure slips she was giving out, found her way to the Dean's Office. She wasn't the only new teacher doing so. I guess it was the shingle on the door reading:

PSYCHOLOGICAL SERVICES

Or was it the other sign?

THE DOCTOR IS IN

"Let's nail this down, Ms. K. Why are you here?"

"My grades look like London during the blitz."

"Interesting analogy."

"I've used enough red inks to paint Red Square."

"That would take one hell of a brush."

"What are you talking about?"

We were back to square one.

"Actually, I don't know."
"I came here for assistance."
"You're not the only one."
"What?"
"Ms. K, is there a topic sentence here?"

That was my very crafty response to the incomprehensible.

"I'm giving too many fails."
"This is about grading?"
"This is about red ink."
"Let's leave the Bolsheviks out of this. What's going on?"

I didn't need an answer. Ms. K wasn't the first young teacher to enter the Dean's Office (make that clinic) about a grading problem. Amend that a bit… We're really talking about evaluating two things, how well the student learned and the flip side, how well we taught. There's a lot involved here.

"I'm giving too many fails. I feel awful about that."
"Why?"
"Why, what?"
"Why is this so hard? Why did you hand out so many fails?"
"Because the students failed."

Talk about circular thinking. The merry-go-round had nothing on us. Just jump on your favorite horse and hang on.

"Ms. K, let's narrow this down. Pretend I'm in your class. What did I do (or not do) to earn a fail?"
"You failed your quizzes and tests."
"Ah, we're getting some place now. Anything else?"
"Very little homework was done."

"And I was a good citizen in class?"

"No. You disrupted my lesson too often."

"What about my attendance, Ms. K?"

"Present most of the time, but often late to class."

"So all and all I'm a charming young fellow?"

"Hardly."

"You alerted the family?"

"Multiple times."

"You talked with the kid?"

"Numerous times."

Grading… It is for many teachers, the most difficult aspect of instruction, and with good reason. You have to design an evaluative instrument (make that test) that — and here's the rub — that actually shows what the student learned (or didn't learn). Then you have to grade the outcome; that is, relate the evaluation to a grade, A to F, or possibly pass, no pass. Of course, you can use a numerical system, 60% (D) to 90% (A). But if you grade on a class average, 90% might be a B+ under some circumstances. Naturally, you might simply list a point total for the semester; achieve 750 points and you'll receive… Of course, for the slow starters that can be the kiss of death. Beyond that there is the question of so-called objective tests (multiple choice) or subjective evaluation (like reading an essay). And on an on we go the merry-go-round turns only we're not in an amusement park.

"I feel so inept when it comes to grading."

"And guilty when you fail so many students, Ms. K?"

"Just terrible."

"Like you failed?"

"Exactly."

"Your subject instructional guides helped?"

"Are you kidding, Dr. Livingston?"

"Your department chair?"

"He tried."

"District specialists?'

"Not much better."

"Your education classes in college?"

"A desert."

"The school administrators?"

"We're off the record?"

It sometimes came down to that question in the Dean's Office. That being the case, I was prepared.

"I am the soul of discretion, plus I have a faulty memory. Not to worry, Ms. K."

"They tried."

"Okay, we're back to a question. Why are you here?"

"I want some real help."

I like to think I have all the answers. Sadly, that's seldom the case. About the best I have is an approach to the problem.

"When it comes to grading most teachers have a 'heel problem.'"

"What?"

"You know the River Styx."

"I ..."

"The Trojan War bit."

"I..."

"You've heard Peleus and Thetis, the parents of Achilles."

"Greek mythology... But how does that help me?"

"Recall what happened to Achilles. His folks tried to make him invulnerable so they dunked him into the waters."

"I know the story."

"Then you know his problem?"

"He was held by his heel, Dr. Livingston."

"And?"

"That left him vulnerable."

"Good, we're done."

"What?"

"As teacher's the educational system held us by our heels. That's why you feel so bad. That's where we're vulnerable. Grading is the great puzzle we're confronting all the time. It challenges us with more questions than answers, and certainly a lot of confusion."

"Confusion."

"Like the IRS and your income taxes. Talk to ten IRS folks about the same tax return and you're probably going to get ten different answers. Okay, do the same with an essay. Ask ten teachers to grade it. Guess what you'll get?"

"Ten answers?"

"Sometimes eleven or twelve, but we won't go into that."

"So what do I do?"

I dislike that question so I equivocate. I make ambiguousness an art form. I tell a story.

The Tower of Babel

"Years ago I had a senior economics class, some 44 students all needing the class to graduate. About twenty of the students were already accepted to fine schools, UCLA, University of Oregon, Arizona State, and yes, USC. The others, if they attended college, would probably go to a community college. Others were headed for vocational school or perhaps the service. Was it academic diversity at its best or worse? It was certainly an academic Tower of Babel. Homogeneity did not reign. Here was the problem? Where should I pitch the instruction and consequently, how should I grade? How could I challenge both groups without doing harm to either one? Too hard, I lose students. Too easy, I'll bore others to death. Where was the middle ground?"

"I can't imagine."

"I tried a number of things (all my instructional tricks), but overall I didn't do well."

"There's a lesson here for me?"

"Yes. Every class is like that even when identified as "gifted," or "average," even in an AP class. There's always a multitude of skill levels in every class. And, of course, each home is different, running the gambit from "a safe, supportive, and protective environment to the dysfunctional where three meals a day and a comforting voice maybe truant. Between these poles are many possibilities."

"So what should I do?"

It was becoming increasingly more difficult to evade Ms. K's question. Certainly, conventional answers conveniently came to mind. Hand out your grading scale the first week of school, but not an elaborate, long-winded syllabus requiring an IBM computer printout. Make it simple. One sheet of paper and review it occasionally. You might even send it home for a parent signature. That forecloses parents arguing, "We didn't know." Naturally, if you're teaching more than one subject, the grading procedure will differ somewhat. This goes under the heading of "variety is the spice of life."

"I already do some of that."

"Well, try this on for size. Provide examples of C, B, and A work. If the class is making a map of the classical Roman Empire, provide examples indicating demarcation lines, coloring, and labeling. That can really help many to improve their grades,"

"That's a lot of work."

"Try it with a short, two-page essay on the meaning of Lincoln's death in1865 if you want to task yourself. Or you can try group work, but rather than simplifying the situation, things could get even more confusing."

"I'm afraid to ask."

"Well, who gets the credit and the better grade. Or is this a Socialist project with a collective grade with the better students pulling others up, or vice versa?"

"I'm not sure you're helping, Dr. Livingston."

I probably wasn't. But here's the deal. Grading in an English class is not like evaluating players on the high school football team. First string is composed of the best athletes based on competition. There will only be one starting QB, the others back him up. The best players will start on defense. A degree of objectivity is possible compared to reading essays. That said, I was going to avoid the comparison. I would fall back on a last ploy. I would throw a "Hail Mary" pass.

"Ms. K, grading is both a technique and an art. Where the two overlap is not always discernable. Over time and with greater experience, you get better at it. Perfection is, I'm afraid, not possible.

"That solves the problem?"

"Sadly, no. It just amplifies it. Just do your best. That's all you can do."

"But I feel so lousy about the fails."

"Back to that again… Then another rather short story."

The Great Truth

Another young English teacher told me this story years ago. It stuck with me. Perhaps it will help you.

The teacher failed a high school senior, causing him not to graduate. Before the semester ended she spoke with him in private.

"Adam, I tried everything to help you. Nothing seemed to work. I would have given you a D- if you had done anything. I just couldn't reach you. I'm so sorry."

"It wasn't your fault."

"That's it, Dr. Livingston?"

"Yes."

"What did she do?"

"She cried a lot and then went on summer vacation."

"But?"

"There is no 'but.' She moved on. She had done the best she could in an imperfect world."

"I should move on?"

"What else is there to do?"

Chapter 21

Smack Time

"God, if I only could do it."

It was a hot, humid September day, the sort of day when the A.C. struggled to keep up with the frying pan heat, and tempers were short. It was the kind of day where nerves were stretched and strained to some unknown but very present breaking point. It was the sort of day where, as a Dean, you might "lose it" because you just wanted to smack some smart-assed jerk, who had pushed your buttons once too often.

"Enough is enough."

No more smooth talk, refined words to color how you really felt. "You know, your teacher has a point, too. You need to look at this from her perspective." No more professional demeanor laced with subtle, suggestive thoughts to help a parent, who was an idiot. "Mrs. Hill, perhaps you should consider family counseling to find out why your three kids are having trouble in school." No more "let's work together" when that meant acceding totally to the absolute power of your boss. "Certainly, Mr. Principal. I completely understand the school policy and you can be assured I will follow it to the letter (even if it is illogical and unenforceable)."

I just hated to be under control all the time.

I strolled around my office. Perhaps pacing was a better way to describe my gait. Little beads of perspiring anger roller-coasted down my neck, drenching my once stiff white collar into a taffy-like substance. I was under control, but I was also really worn out and certainly lacking in patience. My reserves of professional constraint had lapsed. My well-polished cool image had evaporated. Civilized feelings were giving way to the hunter instincts of the jungle.

I could taste blood, and it tasted good.

There was no question about that or any other elegant word to illuminate how I felt. I wanted to hit something hard. I wanted to feel the consoling sensation of my fist striking the soft, tender flesh of that self-satisfied, ignorantly indulgent "somebody," who needed a refreshing "kick in the ass."

In moments like this, I wanted to be *General George C. Patton*. I wanted to slap some miserable slob into a manhood of responsibility and commitment toward something greater than his own mealy-mouthed existence.

At times like this, I wanted to be Vince Lombardi, the Italian dynamo who coached the Green Bay Packers to two Super Bowl victories. He was built like a fire hydrant. He could and did grab bulky 300-hundred pound offensive tackles by their sweaty jerseys and then screamed into their unbelieving faces, "This is the way we do it in Green Bay."

The Walkman Episode

My ticked-off day started before school. A tearful sophomore ran up to me at my supervision gate, crying. "He took my *Walkman* and head phones." As she threw the words at me, she pointed toward a big kid walking away at a fast clip, faster than the usually semi-comatose students walk at that time in the morning. "He just grabbed it out of my hands."

I left my gate and with the near hysterical *Sony* girl followed the accused. As we did, an unabated woeful description of the radio poured out from the girl's soul, ending with a watery comment, "My dad bought it for me. It was my birthday yesterday."

It was at that moment, I think, that I started to lose it.

As we approached the "suspect," he disappeared into a crowd for a moment, and then reemerged with a shy, shit-ass smile on his face. Rather than continuing to walk away from us, he waited while his buddies scrambled away.

"Christ," I yelled a little too loudly, "I know what he did."

The stolen radio had been passed on to someone. There was no question about that. No wonder our suspect was waiting for us. He was clean as a newborn baby's backside.

"Is this the person?" I asked the ever-weeping girl. "Did he take your radio?"

"Yes," she answered in a choking voice. "Yes, he took it."

"This chick has me mixed up with someone else," the accused replied with a smirk.

Click. Another piece of professional control headed south.

I took both students to my office. One went willingly. The other resented my request "to follow me," and yelled very loudly about "racial profiling" and "biased deans," who picked on Hispanic males.

Click. Click. My veneer of civility was fleeing for a safer clime.

Once in the office, a full statement was taken from each in writing. "He did it" was the jest of her anguished words. As expected, denial lathered the suspect's rambling syntax. After sending the young lady off to class with a promise to find her *Sony*, I interviewed "Mr. Loud Mouth."

"Well?" I asked.
"I didn't do it."
"Really?"
"Yeah."
"Why would she accuse you?"
"Stupid mistake. Dumb chick. I told you that before."

Click. Click. Click.

"I don't think so."
"She's confused me with someone else."
"What?"
"You know… Hispanic guys all look the same to white babes."
"I didn't know that."
"It must be our good looks."
"Something in your genes?"
"Why not?"

There was a clicking sound in my chest and the faint taste of blood in my mouth. I could feel the animal in me growing.

"I know you took it. Who has it now?"
"No way, man. Not me… I didn't snatch it."
"Which "homey" has it?"
"That's a racist remark. Just because I'm Hispanic…"
"And all your buddies are Hispanic…"
"See! Racist shit. Go after the Asians. They get away with all kinds of shit in this school"

"But you had the radio, not the Koreans. Not the Chinese. Not the Vietnamese. Just you."

"Prove it, Dean-O," he said with an unbecoming smirk. "Prove it, Mr. Detective."

CLICK!

I was hunting pray now. Blood lust was taking over. The jungle was now everywhere.

I wanted to reach out across the desk and smack the shit-eating grin off his all too contented face. A thought froze in my throat. "I bury you here, kid. You'll never graduate from Van Nuys High." The thought remained frozen.

"If I have to, I'll call in all your buddies."
"Big deal."
"Someone will break."
"Go ahead and do it, Mr. Tough Guy."

CLICK!!

"Rio will be involved."
"Donut man… Who cares?"
"You might before it's over."
"Don't bet on it."

As a teacher, there was always that one kid "you wanted to kill." Of course, you didn't really didn't mean it. You just wanted the kid off your back. At this moment, though, I was all fangs and lathered up for a good fight.

"I could pass the word that you caved in and spilled names."
"Who would believe you?"
"Who wouldn't if I phrased it just right."
"Go ahead. Do your 'white man' thing."

"Perhaps I should just talk with my friends in BVN. They might think you're giving them a bad name."

"I'm tight with BVN."

"Really? Why don't we find out how tight.? Let's find out what the older guys in the barrio think."

"Not their business," he countered but with decidedly less confidence.

"I'll make it their business."

A quiet moment crept into the office. Prowling leopards and tigers were moving silently through the airless tangle of impenetrable bush and vines, which obscured and hid all until the moment to pounce. The silence was thick with deathly anticipation.

"Fine. I'll contact Rio. I'll inform him of what's going down. As of this moment, you're suspended for three days for disrespect and lying, and for making sexist remarks about white girls. I'll call your parents at work and let them know what's happening. I'll recommend a transfer to another school, one far away from Van Nuys, and the same for your friends, all to different schools."

"You can't."

"Try me."

In a fantasy moment, I really wanted to say:

"Let me show you something." I would then phone the Main Office. "Send it over." A few minutes later, by prearrangement, the door opens and the school secretary handed me a flat package. She leaves, but not before saying, "It recorded by time and location."

"I've got a tape here. Do you want to change your story before I play it?"

"You into Disney cartoons?"

"Last chance."

"Donald Duck? Mickey Mouse? What have you got?"

"You, that's what I've got. On film grabbing the Sony."

"Bull."

"You mean toro, don't you? The new cameras at the gates caught you in the act. Isn't that just great?"

"Cameras?"

"Yep. Made by Sony. Can you believe it?"

"No way."

"Apparently, you gave an Osc*ar* performance. Want a peek before I call in Rio?"

Sadly, the school didn't have any cameras. I only had the jungle. It would have to be enough with this kid.

The kid didn't break. I couldn't prove my case. I didn't involve BVN. The girl lost her *Walkman.* Some days are like that.

Collegial Conflict

Teachers can be very frustrating especially the male faculty members who want to demonstrate their masculinity in a zealous, if not foolhardy way, with out-of-class, equally macho muscles belonging to street smart guys. They can be very frustrating.

"Damn, Byron, what were you thinking?"

"He was cutting class."

"I don't care if he was stealing the Queen's jewels. What you did was stupid."

"I couldn't just let him walk away with that shit ass look on his face."

"Yes, you could have and you should have."

Byron was a middleaged math teacher in pretty good shape. He worked out a lot in the school's weight room and had once been a pretty good running back in a small southern college. He liked to "run" into people on the way to T.D. heaven. This particular day, he had almost gotten to the heaven part.

Byron had run into two Hispanic students ditching class. When he asked for their I.D.'s, they gave him lip, then started to run. Byron grabbed one by the shirt and held on. As the kid struggled, whether by accident or intent, he caught Byron with a hard punch or push to the chest, which knocked the teacher to the ground. The kid took off like a NASA rocket.

"You could have been hurt," I exclaimed to Byron.

"This doesn't count?" he replied while rubbing his chest.

"Really hurts?"

"Screw it. No kid mouths off to me."

So typical of some guys … "I'm the authority figure here, the teacher, the adult, and over 21-crowd. Don't fuss with me, or I'll knock you for a loop."

"Listen, Byron, stopping those kids was not the problem."

"Not the problem!"

"No."

"Well, what was?"

"Three things… First, you got in their faces. Second, you touched them. And third, you didn't show them respect."

"Respect!"

"You went kick-ass authority on them."

"Well, Mr. Smarty, what should I have done."

It was at this moment that I first wanted to smack Byron. A nice smack across the face which would leave a ringing sound in his ears. Naturally, I resisted the temptation. Barely.

"Ask them politely why they're out of class. Study their faces as they speak so you can pick them out of our photo book if they run. Remind them without raising your voice that you can do this."

"And, if they run?"

"Pick them out of the photo book and we've got them."

"Chicken shit way to deal with assholes."

Now I really wanted to smack Byron open hand from the right, followed by a backhand from the left. Stupidly, he was going to put himself at-risk to satisfy his "I'm in charge ego." He didn't seem to understand, or didn't want to understand that a kid might just haul off and clobber him if pushed too far. Given the violent streets that these kids come from, the availability of guns, and the wide use of drugs, it was crazy for Byron to act this way. And damn it all, if a kid did hurt him, I would need to arrest the kid and recommend expulsion from the school district over what started as a minor infraction.

It would be so much easier to just smack Byron.

The Uppity Parent

Now as to smacking a parent; the school board frowns on his sort of behavior by its Deans. But boy, would I have liked to do it just once. A little smack, more symbolic than physical, just hard enough to feel a warm tingling feeling in my body, a small moment to enjoy the afterglow of the act and the surprised look on the recipient's face. Oh glory, what a feeling it would be.

"Mrs. Watson, may I speak to you in complete candor?"
"Candor?"
"Yes. Truthfully."
"I guess so."

Dear Mrs. Watson was in the office to talk about her son, Alex. This was the third time in two months. Alex, a senior, was a self-centered smart guy who was letting his last semester become a disaster: cutting classes, doing just enough to get a "D-grade," and making snide, if not satirical remarks in class, which bordered on disrespect but never quite crossed the line.

"Harold tells me you bought him a new car."

"It's a late model BMV."

"You're paying the insurance?"

"Oh, yes. Harold doesn't have a job."

Smack time …

"Why are you doing this? Look at his grades and his behavior in class."

"He needs transportation."

"Let him ride the bus."

"Oh, I couldn't do that."

Smack time…

"Apparently, he's going on a ski trip next week."

"Yes, the whole family is going to Utah."

"Even though he's doing terribly in school?"

"We've been planning this trip for a long time."

Smack time…

"Alex gets $50 per week for allowance, plus gas money?"

"How did you know that?"

"We were comparing salaries. His was larger."

"He has expenses."

"And a drug habit?"

"Alex doesn't do drugs. I've asked him."

"Ask him again."

"I will not."

Smack time…

"I understand Alex is going to a small, private college."

"Yes, a school his father attended."

"Expensive?"

"Very."

"Even with his poor grades?"

"He'll mature."

Smack time...

As I said earlier, we don't smack parents. Denial, as in this case, is a parent prerogative not to be called into question by any Dean. Reality, as determined and defined by the parent, is sacred. No school person dares challenge it. Smack time exists only as a fantasy. You learn that as a Dean. You learn that as a teacher.

Chapter 22

Money

"I feel penniless around this time each month."
"That wealthy?"
"I wish."

I was in my office with a distraught, second year young teacher. Over the years I had earned a reputation with new teachers as someone who could assist them, not just with school problems but also with personal issues. I was sort of like an Ann Landers on campus. Harold had stopped by the Deans Office for financial advice. The *Kiplinger* folks had nothing on me.

"I can barely pay my rent, or the monthly for the beat up loaner I'm driving. I thought being a teacher was a good middle class job."
"Well, it is and it isn't."
"That sure helps."
"I'm a font of clarity (forget the wisdom).

It was a recurring topic. I had heard it before. I would hear it again. It was in the DNA of new teachers (Down to Nothing in Assets). Usually, the conversation went like this:

"I waned to teach. I love kids. I like what I'm doing, but I can't live on my salary. It's a month-to-month fiscal disaster. I feel like an indentured servant, or an all but enslaved tenant farmer. Why did I go to college for five years to become an educated peon in our society? And, as an after thought, my college debt, it's strangling me."

What could I say? The sun will come up tomorrow (sorry Ernest, or was it Annie?). Before I could get into the celestial mysteries of the universe, I had to first deal with the predictable accusation.

"You don't seem to have the same problems, Dr. Livingston. You wear nice suits (off the rack), drive a new car (actually previously owned), and live in a nice neighborhood (that I couldn't afford today)."

"Well, I have an edge on you, Harold, I've been selling grades to students for years."

"You're kidding?"

"Well, actually to their parents."

"That's B.S.!"

"Actually it's illegal, but I've been tempted."

"Come on; how do you do it?"

"Harold, I've been in the district for 35-years. I've been married to a nice lady and fellow teacher for most of that time. That helps… I'm at the top of the teacher pay scale. You're almost at the bottom."

'Was it difficult for you?"

"Harold, you have no idea"

"Tell me."

The Setup

I started teaching in 1962, spring of that year at a local junior high. I graduated from San Francisco State and headed southward to LA. I was a Kennedy kid. You know, "do something for your country." I figured I'd teach. That spring semester I had three World History classes (7th-graders) and two English classes (9th-graders), and, as I would eventually learn, a good many of my students were repeats. Because of attendance and behavioral problems they were dumped into my classes.

Talk about a setup. As to assistance, there wasn't much. As I recall the Head Counselor said:

"Here's the instructional guide for each class. Read it over the weekend."

"Okay."

"Here's a copy of district policies. Make sure you know the 'do's' and 'don't.'"

"Okay."

"Here's your grade book. Two grades each week for each kid. Keep it neat and accurate for the near deranged when they confront your grading system."

"Okay."

"Any questions?"

"Books?"

"The better sets have already been spoken for. You're the low man on the totem pole. The textbook clerk will give you what she can. Any questions?"

"Lesson plans."

"Weekly for review (if anyone cares to look)."

"Assistance?"

"You're on your own dime."

"What does that mean?"

"Just get through each day."

"When do I get paid?"

"In four weeks?"

"I'll starve by then."

"Get a personal loan from the teacher's credit union or see the Principal."

"The Principal!"

"He makes small no interest loans to teachers to tide them over."

"You're kidding?"

All this I explained to Harold. It was a repeating a recurring horror story again and again, sort of like that movie about *Groundhog Day*. I shared this economic calamity with destitute scholars and financially pinched teachers each year.

Surviving Your Pay Check

"So how did you survive?"

"Beans... Hot dogs on sale at *Food Giant*... Generic macaroni and cheese... Peanut butter and jam sandwiches... And foreign aid."

"Foreign aid?"

"Kids would leave little unopened cartons of orange or apple juice at nutrition. I'd collect what I could."

"No way."

"Then the sweet little girls got into the picture. They saw me as an eligible bachelor. I was invited to many homes for dinner and to meet the older sister. The parents were astonished by how much I could eat. As a matter of fact, so was I.

"Dr. Livingston, I don't know what to believe. There's a certain neurotic element to your stories."

Harold was on to me. It was time to share more of my pronounced paranoia personality.

The Elusive Pay Check

"Harold the school districted was my fiscal enemy. I don't think downtown had any intention to pay me. It was all a put on."

"What are you talking about?"

"In the fall and my first year of teaching, I taught for three weeks before I received the first half of my first check. That was almost a month of work for half my pay. Then I taught for two more weeks before the other half appeared, and then I taught for four weeks before the first full check."

"Jesus."

"In my case, Harold, I said, Holy Moses. But, of course, that wasn't the worst of it. There were no checks during the summer. There were only ten checks per year. That's it."

"How did you survive?"

"The power of 12 and the law of selfishness."

"What are you talking about?"

"With only 10 checks, I had to divide by 12 in order to cover each month. Of course, you don't have to do that now. The Teachers Union won the right to monthly checks during the 1970 strike."

"What about this selfishness business?"

"Very simple, Harold. No matter how much (or little) you earn, always pay yourself first through savings and investments. That's your first bill, not your last. Be selfish. Take care of yourself first. You'll live on the remainder. Also, when you get a raise, throw half of the net into savings. Don't spend all of the increase. Does that make sense to you?"

"Yes, but…"

"But what?"

Harold balled his fists. His mouth and jaw tightened. It was obvious he was angry.

"I shouldn't have to do odd jobs during the summer. For god's sake, I'm a college graduate. It's demeaning."

I had heard that one before. I referred to it as the "champagne taste buds and the beer wallet complex."

"Harold, who forced you to be a teacher.?"

"No one. I like working with kids."

"Anyone forcing you to stay in teaching?

"No."

"You saw the salary schedule before you signed up?"

"Yes."

"Well then, what are you complaining about? You knew what you were getting into? You would receive a predictable, very modest salary, befitting a replaceable civil servant. You would also be enrolled in a reasonable health insurance program, and a fair but distant retirement system. What else do you want?"

"Monetary respect. Pay me what I'm worth."

"And that is?"

Harold went silent. I'd heard it before. I want to be valued like a baseball pitcher. Fair enough. When you can throw like one, okay. I want to earn more like a hip-hop singer. Okay, than sing and dance like one. You see where this is going.

"Dr. Livingston, I bet you never had to do odd jobs."

"Harold, my boy, you couldn't be more wrong."

Odd Jobs

If I didn't get a summer school job teaching, I always found something. One summer I drove a school bus for a private camp. I picked up the little dears in the morning and escorted them home in the late afternoon. In the camp I taught swimming though I could hardly swim a lick. Fortunately, we were in three feet of water. Another summer I worked in pre-*Walmart* store. It was called *White Front*. I worked in the sports department selling guns. Imagine me, a pacifist, selling arms like nobody's business. I also sold fishing gear though the only fish I ever caught was filleted, frozen, and at a Safeway store. During the winter break I worked at the Post Office yanking mail sacks out of trucks. At the apartment where I lived, I washed the parking spots to reduce my rent.

"You liked doing that?"

"Not necessarily, but I had to survive, and one job was kind of to my liking."

"Teaching swimming?"

"Working a liquor store after a full day of teaching.

Customers and Counseling

I found a part time clerk's job in a liquor store near the junior high. Worked from 4:30 p.m. to about 10 p.m. three times a week. I did that for about a year. Funny thing about that job; I met a good number of parents whose kids were in my classes. As I think back our conversations went like this.

"That will be $10.50."
"I heard you teach over at the junior high."
"That's correct."
"My kid goes there. He tells me you're his teacher."
"Small world."
"Johnny Thompson."
"Period 3, US History."
"Right."

The next comment always happened. It was reflective of a sort of impromptu Open House, or a 'half-way' house I was running for parents.

"How's he doing? I'm worried about him."
"As I recall, fine. Good kid."
"That's nice to hear."

Even if the kid had been a serial killer, I would have considered saying something positive about him. You can't sell booze to an unhappy father (or maybe you can).

"Any thing I can do to help, call on me."
"I will."

The conversation always ended on an upbeat.

"By the way, we're having a special on Jim Beam next week."
"Thanks."

There's an additional rough edge to this job. The Principal found out about it and spoke to me.

"Dr. Livingston, you're a professional. Do you think this is an appropriate job?"

"Until the Board pays me more, I have no choice. I'm the victim of a conspiratorial fiscal plot to starve me into submission."

"Our parents will hear about this."

"I see them every day. Great customers."

"What will your students think?"

"Hopefully, that I have a great work ethic."

"I hear you visit the bar next door after work."

"True, but only on Friday nights. By then, it has been a long week and I'm in need of Haig and Haig therapy."

"What will people think?"

"I don't know and I'm not sure I care."

The conversation never went far, Harold. You can see that, can't you?"

"Yes, I think so. But what should I do?"

The moment of truth…

"Two winning pieces of advice. If you want to stay in education and make more money, become an administrator. That's where the 'big bucks' are. It seems to be an ironclad rule that the more you make in this business, the less time you have directly with students. If that's not for you, seek out and marry a cute teacher. Reach a deal with her. Live on a check and a half for three years, save the rest for a down payment on a house. In three years you'll prove that two can starve as easily as one on a limited budget, but you'll also have that down payment."

"You did that?"

"It was the best of time and the worst of time."

Chapter 23

Sensitivities

"Jesus, Dr. Livingston, I'm in real trouble now."

"I have a doctorate in trouble. What's going on?"

"Names."

"Names?"

Miss Freelander was in my office. She was in tears. My box of tissue was taking a real beating.

"Miss Freelander, what's going on?"

"I don't know what words to use anymore. It's all so confusing."

"I'm bit confused myself."

"I'm in trouble with the parents."

"I can relate to that."

"I don't know what to call them."

"The parents?"

"No, their kids."

"Use their first name."

"Not that…"

"Okay, their second name."

"No."

"Miss. Freelander, you have to call them something. Perhaps a numerical system would work, or something dealing with their clothes. You appear to be open to lots of choices."

209

"You don't understand."
"On that we agree."

At this point I was beginning to think one of use was certifiable. But then Miss Freelander saved both of us from the guys in white.

"I don't know what word to use. Black, colored, African-American, Negro..."
"I..."
"And then the other group — Native-Americans, First People, Indians?
"I..."
"Hispanics, Mexicans, Latina... It's all so confusing."
"I..."
"Why can't people just have one name?"
Good question, I thought. I now understood where this business was going? That's me, a Dean with an iron-trap mind.

"You're in trouble with some parents?
"They think I'm prejudiced."

Poor lady, she didn't understand she was living in the age of *Ivory* soap. For the young generation, I'm referring to a jingle — *99, 44, 100% Pure* — that sold millions of little white bar of scrubby soap.

I explained my Ivory soap theory. All around us our "purists," people who believe they have an insight to absolute truth, to an inviolate truth, to a self-justifying truth, to a truth that gives them structure, predictability, and security. You're seeing a mild form of it when it comes to group names.

"What should I do?"
"Check with the District's equity people. Find out the latest acceptable names. Check in now and then to keep up with changes. That's about all you can do."

"What if the kids or parents object to my choice?"

"Tell them to sue the Board of Education."

"Really?"

"Really."

Miss Freelander seemed satisfied with my answer. Unfortunately, I wasn't. That said, I felt compelled to amplify.

"Another thing... The flip side of Ivory purity is political correctness, an ugly and inexpensive form of intellectual thinking. You see it everywhere. People hold up their 'what-should-I-know?' finger in the air to find out what the current, acceptable view is, which they then adopt. This keeps you with the 'in-group.' This avoids straining your 'little brain cells.' This assures you'll never be in the minority. Political correctness requires no effort on your part to rigorously think through an issue independent of the mutterings of the crowd."

"I don't understand. How does that affect me as a teacher?"

"What you say. The topics you bring up in class. The views you share with your students, all treacherous little Claymore land mines waiting to blow up in your face. In this regard, you're constantly censoring yourself to avoid upsetting someone. Believe me, I know."

"You got into trouble, but you're the Dean."

"I'm an experienced 'get into trouble guy.'"

"Hard for me to believe."

"Fortunately, I can't show you the scars on my backside. This is a 'G-rated' Deans Office, but permit me to make one thing abundantly clear. Not all parents want their kids freely and openly discussing certain things in the classroom. This is particularly true in history and government classes, the classes you teach. I'd like to give you an example from my own experience.

The Second Bomb

"It all started out so innocently. It always does, I'm afraid. I gave my government class an assignment. Pick any topic in American history and explain and defend the prevailing and accepted interpretation related to the topic."

"Sound like a good assignment. Maybe I will use it."

"Okay with me. No royalties involved, but bend an ear first."

"I'm bent."

"I suggested a few topics:

. Columbus sails to the New World – Good or bad deal for Europe and the World?
. Jefferson scribbles the Declaration of Independence – Good or bad deal for the rebellious colonials?
. Teddy Roosevelt constructs the Panama Canal – Good or bad deal for the US and our relations to Latin America?

"And then there was the topic that really hit the fan:

. Dropping the second atomic bomb on Nagasaki — Good or bad for Japan?

Boy, did that one light a fuse. First, there was the mother who wanted to know where the answer was in the book.

"There's no simple answer in the book."

"Which book should my son use?"

"He needs to do research. He'll use a few books, and other sources."

"But what's the answer?"

"There's no one answer. This is research, analysis, and interpretation."

"If there's no right answer, why give the assignment?"

There was no way I could satisfy this parent, or the local Japanese Cultural Center representative who sought me out.

"Are you saying the second bomb shouldn't have been dropped?"

"I'm not saying anything."

"You're opposed to the use of the atomic bomb?"

"For the purpose of this assignment, I'm not taking a position."

"Do you have a hidden agenda."

"If so, I can't find it."

"You're being flippant."

"I'm being flippant because the questions are inane."

"You're harboring anti-Japanese feelings?"

"Only those at Pearl Harbor."

Well, again you can see we were getting nowhere. The same thing happened when I received a phone call from the local VFW contingent.

"VFW?"

"Veterans of Foreign Wars, a fraternal group of ex-service people."

"What did they want?"

"My unpatriotic head for starters."

"Why?"

"I was calling into question the use of the 'gadget' on Hiroshima and Nagasaki. I couldn't convince him otherwise. Pretty soon the Principal was getting rabid phone calls from disgruntled citizens and soon I was in his office explaining my nefarious assignment. Eventually, things worked out and the kids did excellent work. Of course, I didn't give that assignment again (in the same form) for a few years. I found other ways to accomplish my goals in more subtle ways. At heart, I was a Darwinian. I had to adapt and evolve to survive in the 'politically correct jungle.'"

"That's quite a story."

"Isn't it? But there's still another shoe to fall."

Defensive Driving

We're all accustomed to the concept of defensive driving. Watch out for the other guy. Use your signals before changing lanes. Watch the space between cars and your speed. You know the drill. Now apply the same practices to education.

"I'm not sure I understand you."
"Miss Freelander, some examples, if I may."

Examples

I'm driving home after school in a driving rain. I see a student I know sloshing through torrents of water. Do I stop and offer him a ride? In the past I did. But today, no...

I'm in my office (or your classroom) I'm alone with a student. Do I shut the door completely for privacy? In the past, yes... But not these days, not on a bet...

A student invites me to her home for dinner with the family. Do I accept the invitation? Once upon a time, of course... Today, probably not...

A kid wants to discuss a very personal matter. Do I agree? Yes, but only after providing cover for my credential. "Look, we can talk, but you have to understand something. If we get into certain subjects, I have to make a report. If we move in that direction I'll give you the high sign."

The student is in tears, a one-person Yosemite Falls and in need of a hug. What do I do? It's impossible to hug without touching unless you're into mysticism. But touching can be misconstrued. At one time, I hugged. Now I keep my distance, painful as it can be.

What do all these examples have in common? You got it: SEX, the biggest little word and headache in any school. What is a perfectly normal response to assist another human being is now froth with danger. A happy teen receiving a hug might turn it into something else later. Hugging is okay on the athletic field, out in the open and visible to all. In the school hallway, that's another thing. That's the mess we've gotten ourselves into in a world of self-indulgence, combined with litigation attorneys, and folks looking for payout.

"If what you say is true, what do I do?"

"Miss Freelander, in middle and high schools, you exercise caution and beg off to avoid a potentially risky situation. It's a painful sort of risk assessment you entertain to protect your credential. Oh, I wish that it was otherwise."

Miss Freelander left my office. Had I helped her? There was no way to know. There are times when I'm not even sure I can help myself.

Chapter 24

Legacy

I wonder if anyone will remember me, the old Dean with the quixotic personality and bizarre sense of humor, and a somewhat naïve Don Quixote complex. That's the way I saw myself; I was an idealist and romantic bestowed on the world by his astrological sign. I was an Aquarius, an apostle of peace and harmony. That's what the Zodiac proclaimed, but not what I always experienced struggling with the troublesome windmills dotting the landscape of my professional life. What would be my legacy? The question slipped into my consciousness as retirement approached. What did I want people to really remember? Two possibilities eventually emerged.

Nancy's Challenge

"I'm not cut out to be a teacher!"
"A rather harsh assessment."
"But true."
"Only in the heat of the moment, Nancy."

I was in the Dean's Office with a beautiful, talented math teacher who was despairing of her life as a teacher. She had found her way to the on-campus shrink seeking advice.

"I can earn more money in the private sector. Mathematicians are in high demand."

"Especially bright and charming ones from Iran who understands the Middle East mindset, history and culture, those sorts of things. No question, you would bring value to any company."

"Dr. Livingston, are you talking me into leaving?"

"Not in the least, but I am accepting reality. You've had it with the classroom and other pastures look greener. Perfectly understandable... Been there myself."

"You?"

"Sure, I wasn't immune from the seven year occupational itch."

"I don't understand."

This terrific but frustrated teacher wasn't aware of the stage play or movie. I guess they weren't big hits in Teheran. So here I was with a delightful young teacher who had fled the revolution with her family, majored in math at UCLA and now was seriously considering an early exit from the school campus. She had come for advice, but what could I tell her? And more importantly, what did she want to hear? That was the real challenge.

The Beckoning Booze Business

"About eight years into my career, the itch struck with vengeance. Suddenly, I was tired of working for peanuts, putting up with bureaucratic knuckleheads, neurotic parents and their offspring, not to mention the self-proclaimed, idiotic critics of public education. I figured I better get out while I was still a young man with prospects, or at least with my marbles. You know, sort of like you, I think."

"What did you do?"

"I huffed and puffed and one day I saw an ad: liquor store for sale. I was immediately attracted to the possibilities."

"You knew something about the liquor business?"

"Almost nothing. I had worked for a liquor chain in San Francisco while going to college, stocking, clerking, driving, and getting drunk on the job."

"What?"

"It wasn't my fault. It was California's. A rather large earthquake hit and the city 'rocked, rattled, and rolled.' In the store bottles swayed against safety guides lines and then toppled over to begin an anti-climactic dash to the hard floor. Imagine, if you will, a concoction of Napa Valley wine, Scotch from Edinburgh, Kentucky bourbon, vodka from Moscow, plus gin from the UK, and Irish whiskey from Dublin, all floating ankle high on the store floor. It was an international nightmare."

"I can't imagine."

"I had to clean up that mess. By the time I got home, I was flying high. I was looped. My father thought I was drunk, my protestations to the contrary."

"Any other experiences?

"Two. I worked part time in a liquor store to supplement my teacher salary, and I consumed the stuff on more than one occasion, and sometimes more than I should have."

"In the end you…"

"I didn't buy the store. After a pro and con risk assessment, I declined to be my own boss. Two many problems… Being away from the family on holidays, no long vacations as a family, terrible night working hours, and, of course, the ever-present danger that a jacked up guy on drugs might decide to rob the store. In the end I preferred the 'devil I knew.'"

Mirror, Mirror

"So what's really going on, Nancy?"

"The boys in class are making my life miserable. They don't seem to respect me. I can't control them, especially the older ones from my part of the world."

"Even after our earlier talk?"

"Better, yes."

"But not enough?"

"I love teaching. I want to stay in the profession."

"Perhaps I can suggest something."

"Please."

What could I possible suggest? On reflection, one thought did come to mind.

"Show me your teacher face."

"What?"

"Let me hear your teacher voice."

"I…"

"This may help. In your arsenal of 'what-to-do strategies' you need to develop your teacher voice and face so please stand up and look at that mirror."

"You're not kidding?"

"Look at the mirror and show me the face of a justifiably upset teacher."

She did only she couldn't stop laughing as she did so.

"A little sterner look might be better. You know, a 'I'm ticked off at you kid' look."

She tried again and again she laughed.

"I can't do it."

"Alright, look at the mirror and say 'I'm appalled by your behavior in your meanest voice."

She tried. That was about it. I needed an 'ace in the hole.'

"Okay, ever go out on a date?"

"Of course."

"Ever been stood up?"

"Yes!"

"How'd you feel?"

"Lousy!"

"Look at the mirror. See that 'stood up face?' That's your teacher face. When you said 'lousy' that was your teacher voice. Next time a kid is out of control, assume you're looking at that rotten louse, that brigand who ruined your evening. Got it."

"I think so. Will it help?"

"It's a good start. Kids need to know when you're upset. Your look and voice can send a message. 'I'm your worse nightmare if you don't get right with me.'"

Nancy stayed in teaching as far as I know. We lost contact after I retired. I would like to think she recalls me from time to time. That would be a nice legacy.

The Kid

"I have to tell you something."

"Okay."

"Can we go into your office?"

"For privacy?"

"Please."

The young man was distraught. That was obvious. Physically, he seemed a bit frail, like he might break if pushed too hard. He had been a teacher assistant for me last semester. He was a nice kid, really smart with ambitions to be an attorney. As I recall he was a member of he Sierra Club and into environmental issues. A very sensitive soul...

We sat down in my office.

"Okay, what's up, Joseph?"

"I need to talk to someone."

I nodded.
"I trust you."

Again, I nodded.

"I'm gay."

I was prepared for a lot of things, but not that admission. Naturally, I knew that how I responded would be important. I took my time before replying.

"So."
"You're not upset with me?"
"Why should I be?"
"Some people consider it sinful."
"I don't."
"My parents can't handle it."
"You've told them?"
"No."
"You're going to?"
"I don't know. My mom might understand."
"But not your father?"
"Yeah."

There was not much advice in my non-existent *Being a Dean for Dummies* book on how to handle this situation. I was flying on my own.

"Eventually, you'll tell them."
"My dad will kick me out of the house."
"Possibly."
"I'll be on my own."
"Likely."
"I'm scared."
"Understandable."
"What will I do?"

"Survive."

"How?"

"Dig deep. Go to college. Get your law degree."

"Won't be easy."

"What is?"

I needed to help this likeable kid. But what could I say? It was time for me to dig deep.

"Joseph, let me tell you about another young man who was dealt a tough hand. His story just might help you."

"Who?"

"Just a guy I've come to know pretty well."

"Years ago this guy ran away from his home. He was only 17 at the time and still in high school. He left an unhealthy situation that included emotional turmoil, a lot of physical stuff, and certainly an atmosphere not conducive to academics. He left his home without even a 'Goodbye.'"

"Things must have been pretty bad."

"More than you can imagine. I asked him if he did a pro's and con's checklist before leaving? He hadn't. Didn't even pack a suitcase. He had no money, nothing. He had recently lost his part time job. To make matters worse, he was barely passing his senior year. He was close to being a dropout."

"He had a lot on his plate."

"Get this, he was also in trouble with the police for assault and battery and had spent a few days in juvenile hall."

"What happened to him?"

"On the streets of San Francisco for a few weeks living with a friend and his mother."

"Then?"

"At his friend's urging, he went to see his father unsure what that might lead to: 'Come in, or scram.'"

"What happened?"

"His father opened the door with certain conditions."

"Conditions?"

"After graduation in a couple of weeks, the kid could (a) go to work; (b) go to college or vocational school; or (c) see the Navy recruiter."

"What did he do?"

"Going to work was okay, but he had no real skill. His high school grades seemed to eliminate college. Possibly he could go to a vocational school. As to the Navy, that was okay if nothing else worked out."

"And?"

"He made a deal with his father. He would try college for one semester, City College of San Francisco. If he couldn't cut the mustard, he'd join the Navy. His father accepted the deal."

"What happened to him?"

"He did okay in the community college. Got his A.A. degree. Then he matriculated to San Francisco State. Got a B.A. in history, and a year later his teaching credential. He taught in a high school as I recall."

"Do you ever see him?"

"Daily."

Joseph, of course, was caught off guard by that acknowledgment. It took him a moment to collect his thoughts.

"I never knew that about you."

"We've each shared thoughts known but to us."

"And there's a lesson for me?"

"I hope so."

"Keep on fighting?"

"Yes."

"Things will work out?"

"They do, one way or another."

Years later Joseph caught up with me. He was now an attorney. He had survived. He said a lot to me that day, but it all came down to this: "Thanks for being there." It was enough.

As far as I see it, if I'm in the collective memories of Nancy and Jeff, I didn't have to fret about my legacy.

Chapter 25

Farewell

"It's almost time," Jenks reminded me.

I was in my office with Rio and Jenks. There was only one day left in the school year. There were only two days left in my school career spanning 37-years, 1962 through 1999. JFK was President when I started and Bill Clinton held the Oval Office as I was leaving.

"Everyone knows his responsibilities today?" Jenks quizzed. He was being like a mother hen. We had supervised the seniors practicing their graduation walk for many years. We knew our assignments.

My job was simple, yet challenging. I would lead 650 students from the quad area into the football stadium to assigned seats. The line had to be exact and no graduate could be out of order as names were called on that basis. The line had to look good, too. Military precision was not necessary. On the other hand, *Times Square* on New Years Eve was not quite what we had in mind.

"Let's do it," Rio commanded in his best LAPD voice.

We headed for the quad; each of us was alone with his own thoughts. As for me, a sort of career mortality was looking square in my face. This was it. This was my last graduation as a teacher, or Dean. Another day and I would be gone, a footnote, another old guy who had finally retired, another candidate for *Del Webb,* another prospect for salesmen selling annuities, and another "early bird" senior. Ugh. The list was endless and depressing. Sure, I looked forward to retirement, but now reality of it was beginning to sink in, smothering me in its finality.

Of course, I was not privy to what Rio and Jenks were thinking as I left them, but retrospectively, I had a pretty good idea following the next day's ceremony.

"It's arranged?" Jenks asked in a subdued voice.

"Completely."

"The student leaders are organized and ready. The word has been passed."

"Won't he be surprised?"

"The kids were going to do something, even before we got involved," Rio added with a smile.

"Nice. The Principal?"

"In the dark, oblivious."

"Let's keep it that way."

Graduation Day

I was at the head of the graduation line. Mr. Mendoza, always on cue brought his raised arm down as the orchestra, already seated in the football stadium, commenced the graduation ritual. With that, we started walking from the quad toward a large field adjacent to the stadium, where the lines would get their final check before the grand entrance. All went well. The line was reasonably straight and the students somewhat serious as we reached the field. Once there, we stopped.

"It's time," Jenks said.

We entered the football field. The students took their appointed seats. Names were called. Parchment was presented. Things were working without a hitch.

Toward the end of the graduation ceremony, the Principal recognized the teachers who were retiring. As a group, we were sitting on a platform next to the administrators. One at time, our names were called. I was the last of seven retirees. Polite applause greeted those called before me. Then my name was called. To my utter disbelief, the entire graduating class stood and gave me a rousing reception (or sendoff). It went on for at least two minutes before the Principal quieted the *"Class of 1999."*

It was for me a moment never to be forgotten. I had survived the happiness and the sadness, the ironic and the comic, the insane and the inane. It was time to go.

As I stood there, my eyes moistened and an invisible tear found its way down my cheek. It was my moment to quietly hear those special words, my own *"Goodbye, Mr. Chips."*

A Few Words

My career, however, was punctuated by numerous misadventures for which I, as I must, take full responsibility. Perhaps it was my personality … I was always a bit of a rebel in a school world emphasizing bureaucratic conformity and instructional orthodoxy, which, as I saw it, fostered intellectual rigidity. Truth be told, I was a modest risk-taker, who needed to challenge the establishment on occasion out of fear of drowning in a sea of institutional feathers. In short, I pushed the envelope at times.

Retrospectively, the stories I share in these pages represent the contrasting themes of my school career — joy in the classroom bedeviled by non-conformist behavior. What enabled me to survive, I think, was my sense of humor. Somehow, no matter what was happening, I found levity in the human condition — a moment when I could laugh in the face of tragedy, smirk at the antics of people taking themselves all too seriously, or giggle at the gaggle of justifications used to explain human behavior. For me, the school world had a funny bone.

The stories, which follow are representative of my career, especially as a dean. Every event actually occurred, which is not to say that accuracy has not given way to dramatization in my effort to extol the human spirit, whether on a joyous or tragic day.

As to how well I have done this, I will leave that to the reader.

2009
Northridge, California

Printed in the United States
by Baker & Taylor Publisher Services